I0611967

Pa-Pro-Vi Presents…

Our Journey From Boys To Men

Anthology

Things we learned along the way!

Cover Design by LaQuita Parks

Editing by Donnetta Booker

Our Journey From Boys To Men
Things We Learned Along The Way!

The body of work titled Our Journey From Boys To Men Things We Learned Along The Way, Copyright © 2024 by Pa-Pro-Vi Publishing

Cover Design by LaQuita Parks

No part of this publication may be reproduced, stored in a retrieval system, or transmitted in any form or by any means, electronic, mechanical, photocopying, recording, or otherwise, without the written permission of the publisher. the only exception is brief quotations in printed reviews.

For information regarding permission, contact Pa-Pro-Vi Publishing @ www.paprovipublishing.com.

ISBN: 978-1-959667-46-9

Malcolm Bowden~ Robert Brooks
Johnny Brown ~ Marvis Cox
Brandon Darrington ~ Donald Davis
Kevin Eastman ~ Henry Eberhart
Lweendo Handia ~ Julius Jackson
Kelvin King ~ Dean Lillard
Bob Mackey ~ Jeremy Myers
James Parks ~ David Patterson
Dommartini Salien Sr. ~ Curtis Tanner
Kevin Vaughan ~ Anthony Wallace

Table of Contents

20+ men from all walks of life share their stories of things they learned on their journey to becoming a man.

These stories radiate strength, hope, and wisdom. They can give people who are struggling with life's challenges the necessary tools to navigate their trials and tribulations.

From the preacher to the street hustler...these are their stories!

Acknowledgement

I would like to say a sincere thank you to the men who took the time to contribute there stories to this anthology. 100% of everybody living and dead has a story but not everyone has the courage enough to share their story.

FOREWORD

Robert Brooks

I am elated and honored to write this foreword because, for decades, I have had a personal and spiritual relationship with the publisher. We met by chance in the negative; nevertheless, over time, our relationship became so positive that we forgot the negative start.
It didn't take long before we discovered that we were logical and critical thinkers, and our relationship blossomed from that point forward.

LaQuita Parks qualifies to publish this book because she has invested herself in the art of publishing, and it's her passion. LaQuita always views situations with the thought of improving them by investing her mind, soul, strength, and heart correctly and completely to make them a success.

Although LaQuita cannot personally testify to what is

required to journey from a boy to a man, she can know what's necessary to grow into a responsible adult. I know of no human being who has accomplished this better than LaQuita.

I have read and own several of LaQuita's literary masterpieces, all of which reflect her mature, studious writing. I'm blessed to be associated with her and to have my name in the same conversation as LaQuita.

This book project is no different from the bevy of projects she founded. All the authors who contributed to this book are blessed to be part of this endeavor. It's a book about moving forward with a sound purpose to accomplish success in life.

The readers will experience the joy of reading this book because of LaQuita Parks, the founder and CEO of Pa-Pro-Vi Publishing company.

This book is about life and the journeys men make from boys to men. Life is a wise teacher if the student is cognitive and purposefully attentive.

From boys to Men is more than about reaching the age milestone, but more about navigating through the plethora of voices on the landscape of life. It's about having the cognitive mindset to acquire knowledge and being studious enough to decipher the sound from the unsound. It's learning to be a critical and logical thinker on the childhood journey of ignorance to the adulthood of wisdom.

There is only one road from boys to men; nevertheless, there are a plethora of peripheral distractions that can cause one to lose purpose and focus. I believe that this book, properly consumed and digested, will be of utmost importance to those who have not fully matriculated from boys to men.

In some remarkable instances, the publisher has broken new ground, which will bring much satisfaction to the students, the author, and the readers through new thoughts.

The literary style of this work is highly gratifying. The reader (s) does not have to dig through a lot of superfluous verbiage to get to the thought. It is pointed right at your heart in a straight line. Here is a book you will want, buy, and cherish

Introduction

Ms. Queenie Clem- The Literary Ambassador

From Boys to Men: The Essential Role of Knowledge and Wisdom

The path from boyhood to manhood is a transformative journey, marked by a series of trials and triumphs. As we navigate this path, one of the most crucial elements that guide us is the combination of sound information and the wisdom to apply it. This article delves into the stories of brave men from various walks of life who share their experiences and insights, shedding light on the importance of knowledge and wisdom in their journey from boys to men.

- **Understanding the Value of Knowledge:** Growing up, we often hear the adage, "Knowledge is power." This rings especially true for young men transitioning into adulthood. The stories of these men highlight how acquiring sound information—whether through formal education, mentorship, or personal experiences—provided them with the tools they needed to make informed decisions and navigate life's challenges.

- **Applying Wisdom in Everyday Life:** Knowledge alone is not enough. The wisdom to apply this knowledge in practical, meaningful ways is what truly shapes our journey. These men recount moments where they faced critical decisions and how their ability to use wisdom—gleaned from mentors, life lessons, and introspection—helped them overcome obstacles and achieve their goals.

- **Lessons Learned:** Each story is a testament to the power of learning and applying wisdom. From overcoming personal struggles to achieving professional success, these narratives serve as a powerful reminder that the journey from boys to men is paved with continuous learning and the judicious application of what we learn.

As we reflect on these stories, it becomes clear that the journey to manhood is not just about physical growth but also about mental and emotional maturation. Sound information and wisdom are our guiding stars, helping us navigate the complex terrain of life. Embrace this journey with a thirst for knowledge and the discernment to use it wisely.

Why Different?

Malcolm Bowden

Early in the morning, as I catch the school bus, all I hear is my classmates saying, "Hi, Webster." After an adventurous school day, while on my way home, here comes the "What you talkin' about, Willis?" This is in reference to Arnold Jackson, aka Gary Coleman. As the years rolled by, I became accustomed to the chants and nit-picking and, every night, crying myself to sleep with no identity of myself. Growing up in a religious, military household, I didn't have the liberty to speak to the person who is the most important part of my life about being teased or bullied by MY FATHER.

My mother taught us to keep our heads down, not to make eye contact, and your only response should be "Yes sir, nor sir, yes ma'am, or no ma'am." Rejected by my peers for being a "church kid" took its toll on me, my self-esteem, and my self-confidence. Wanting to fit in and be welcomed was a task I gladly accepted, doing and saying anything to grab attention, whether good or bad.

Good for me, I had begun playing organized baseball, and I was pretty good. However, this young black teenager from the Westside found his God-given talents take him to the Eastside of town. A whole new world; as my baseball team continued winning, we found ourselves on our way to the Little League World Series in Texas. That was precisely when my insecurities introduced me to Mr. Budweiser.

I had just gone 7 for 7 in the last 2 games, yet with a headache because of my first blind date with Mrs. Hangover. As we celebrated our clinching victory, I got into a teammate's SUV on the passenger side, and for some reason, I challenged myself to open the door to see if I could jump out and land on my feet while the car was still moving. The reality is that I was overcome by 16 years of being bullied, hampered by inadequacies, and having no value or understanding of my own self-worth.

The two months in recovery, seeing black, white, red, yellow, and brown people affected by this trauma was depressing. A depression led me to have other "dates" in my life with a lady named Hennessey, Mary Jane, and Ms. Sexual Promiscuity. These dates seemed fun for a short time but never fulfilling. While still dealing with self-esteem and self-confidence issues, now I'm struggling with an identity crisis.

Who am I? A drunk? A weed head? Maybe I'm a sexaholic? I would always wake up in the morning at 4:06 am to say a prayer of thanks to God for seeing another birthday. This unique day would be my 38th birthday. As I was praying, a light bulb clicked on within my soul, and with the light came understanding.

I was created to be different. As many people remembered my suicide attempt and how it affected their lives negatively, my testimony is I'm a miracle. I had survived a traumatic brain injury with no side effects, just a few scars. Those same people five minutes later have given their lives to Jesus Christ because this person with no self-esteem, self-confidence, or self-worth and insecurities held onto the only thing worth holding onto in life,

HIS FAITH IN GOD

Why different?...That's why!

About Malcolm

Malcolm Bowden served twenty years as mail clerk and union steward at the United States Postal Service.

Malcolm says, "I'm a servant not a celebrity!"

Malcolm is an Ordained Elder, State license minister, Certified chaplain and other volunteer services.

Malcolm is inspiring and innovative. He is the Founder of MenExcellence Mentorship. He is an author and actor.

Connect with Malcolm:

Facebook: Malcolm J. Bowden

Instagram: mj_greenleef

YouTube: Malcolm Bowden

Email: mjbowden1980@gmail.com

Johnny, "Sometimes We Just Have To Hope Them Out"

JOHNNY BROWN

I was born in 1958 in Milledgeville, Georgia, the 2nd child of seven children to Joseph and Betty Ruth Brown. My Dad was the 21st child of 22 children born to my Grandparents, whom I never got to know as they passed when I was a child! My Mother also had 16 brothers and sisters, and her parents also passed when I was a baby!

From my earliest memories, family and Church were important in our lives. Many of my Dad and Mom's brothers and sisters moved to Detroit, Michigan, and Pompano Beach, Florida. I remember that at least twice a year, our Dad would drive the entire family to visit our aunts and uncles in the North and South!

Our parents taught us how to sing as soon as we could talk, and we always had to sing wherever we would go! Even though none of us were twins, our parents dressed the four boys and the three girls alike as well! The first song we learned was: "You Ought to Take The Lord With You Everywhere You Go"! It was our parents' way of instilling the most important life lesson we would ever learn!

My Father was a Brick Mason by trade. He could do anything involving carpentry, plumbing, building porches, and cement work; yes, he could do anything! Dad would always take us with him when he would go out to work and teach us how to make a living with our hands. Whenever there was work to be done in the community, they called on my Dad! My Mom also taught all of us to cook at an early age, and she made the best Sweet Potato pies in the World! Mom could make a meal out of anything, and we never went to bed hungry!

For the first 10 years of my life, we went to school in Milledgeville, where we were born. We had to catch the bus to school as we lived out in the country! In 1968, they started de-segregating the schools, and we were now being bused to an all-white School! The bus driver who had dropped us off at the Black Schools for years now had to drop us off at the same school his children attended!

We got along great with the teachers and students in this new environment. As a matter of fact, the White teachers were amazed at how good we were doing in class! At recess, the kids always picked my older brother Joseph and me first to be on their teams because we were fast. Well, at least Joseph was fast! About five weeks into the semester, we came home from school, and my Dad was so upset! When we asked him what was wrong, he told us that we were going to have to find somewhere else to live! This was the first time as a child that I experienced racism!

We had been renting the house we lived in from a relative of our White Bus Driver. They told our Dad that immediately our rent was going up from $75.00 a month to $300.00 a month. Our parents said in the words of another song they taught us: "The Lord Will Make A Way Somehow!" God did just that as one of our cousins rented us a house in the next County over, and we moved to Sparta, Ga. While we did not understand it, we all had to change schools, and our parents taught us to love and not hate no matter what came our way!

My Father was not able to finish High School, but he knew math and measurements like nobody's business! He was a Deacon at the Church, and they always took us to Sunday School every week. After Church, which was sometimes all day long, Dad and Mom would take us with them as they went to visit those who didn't make it to Church because they were ill or just down on their luck. Dad would ask if there was any work they needed to be done around the house, and

Mom would take them food; of course, we had to sing for them all!

Later, Dad and Mom started doing Wednesday night Bible study and prayer meetings at home. They soon began taking the Prayer Meeting to the Sick and Shut-in members' houses, and we even visited the Senior Facilities and Youth Prisons to sing and pray with them! My Dad was the strongest Man I knew, but I remember seeing him cry when they killed President Kennedy and Martin Luther King Jr.! Dad took us to March with him when they started marching to change things in Sparta. He taught us that because others had died to help us, we needed to get involved wherever we could! "Johnny, Sometimes We Just Have to _Hope_Them Out"

We now lived on a farm my cousin owned, and my Dad taught me the importance of always working to improve things. I began helping my cousin do everything from picking cotton to pulling watermelons! I worked all summer long on the farm, plowing, cutting okra, harvesting corn, picking peas, tomatoes, and watermelons!

At the end of the week, we would load the truck and go to town to sell what we had grown on the farm. Once we got to town, I would yell out: "Hey Ho the Georgia Plowboy here, we got Collard Greens and Butter Beans, we got fresh tomatoes and sweet potatoes, we got Corn and Peas that are sure to please, and we got Watermelons!" (I did not know that this would lead me to a career in the Grocery business). When I was not working on the farm, I was working with my Dad. Dad would build porches and underpin trailers with blocks, he would pour cement driveways and build rooms on people's houses. My brothers and I would have to dig these long ditches and mix the cement as my Father skillfully would make magic with his hands! We built a huge porch and poured a brand-new driveway for the older couple, and it was the hottest summer I could remember!

My hands had become callused from pushing the wheelbarrow and mixing the cement. Still, I was okay because, in the end, I knew we would make a huge payday! When we finished, it was finally payday, and I remember Dad telling them what he had spent and what he was charging to do all that work. My eyes gleamed with excitement, knowing that this would be our biggest check ever!

The couple looked at my Dad and said, "Joe, we are sorry, but we don't have any money to pay you right now!" My Dad said, alright, and we put all the tools in the car and headed home. As we were pulling off, I looked at my Dad and said I can't believe that we did all of this work, and they did not pay you anything! My Dad looked at me and said: "*Johnny, sometimes we just have to Hope Them out!*" Looking back over my life, I realize that the lessons I learned that summer have helped me become the Man I am today!

"Baseball Has Been Very, Very Good To Me"

I first remember wanting to play baseball after my Dad took me to a game one Sunday afternoon. I had never seen my Dad practice or play at all. They asked my Dad to go into the game, and he played 2nd base. My Dad came up to bat three times, got three hits, and became my inspiration to play baseball! I went out for the team in the 7th grade, and I wanted to be a Pitcher. The coach told me to throw a couple of pitches to the catcher. I wound up and threw the 1st two balls over the backstop! The coach stopped me, gave me a book, and told me to read it and learn how to pitch, and I did not make the team! I did not make the team until the 11th grade.

Our team made the playoffs in my senior year, and we had a chance to make it to the State Playoffs. We won the 1st game of the double header, and I was scheduled to pitch the 2ndgame. The same coach who had given me the book in the 7th grade decided to let the pitcher who had won the 1st game start the 2nd game also! I was devastated, and we gave up 5 runs in the 1st inning and lost the game 5 to 4! I did not get to pitch at all that day! After the season ended, I was going to Voorhees College on a Baseball Scholarship.

The coach from Clark College came down to sign five of my teammates for scholarships at Clark. "Coach Mixon saw me that morning and asked what my name was? He asked if I was a Pitcher, and I said yes, sir! He said why aren't you coming to Clark? I said, "Well, you are not giving me a Scholarship!" He told me to come to the signing. I did, and he also gave me a scholarship. As fate would have it, the other 4 players ended up at Vorhees, and I am the only one who finished at Clark! ("The Lord Will Make a Way Somehow")

I played for 4 years at Clark and was the MVP in my Junior and Senior years. I majored in Mass Communications because, in my way of thinking, I would play Professional Baseball and then retire and become a Radio & TV Sportscaster! I began going to the Major League tryout camps and playing Semi-pro Baseball. One day, one of my college friends called me and told me he had a job.

When I asked him where he said he was working at Kroger! I told him that I did not go to college to end up at a grocery store! I told him I was not interested! Since graduating with honors, I decided I could easily get a job at one of Atlanta's many Radio and TV stations! Well, none of the stations would hire me because they said I did not have any experience! After six months of not getting drafted and not getting hired, I called my friend at Kroger and asked if they were still hiring?

"Paper or Plastic? Everybody's Got to Eat"

Not wanting to go back home and wanting to stay close to the Semi-pro Teams, I swallowed my pride and took a job at the "Disco Kroger" in Buckhead so none of my friends on the South side of town would see me! The only job they had available was bagging groceries, making $3.35 an hour! During my first week at Kroger, my check came to about $75.00, but I made $150.00 in tips! During my second week at Kroger, I made over $250.00 in tips! In my 3rd week at Kroger, I made over $300.00 in tips! In my 4thweek at Kroger, they promoted me to cashier, and I could not make tips anymore!

I was mad and asked them if I could go back to bagging, please? They would not let me do that, so I worked as a cashier for three months, moved to overnight stock for three years, and ran the Frozen Food department for a year before becoming the Receiving Clerk. So, I was playing Semi Pro baseball, working at Kroger, throwing an evening paper route and Umpiring Little League Baseball Games!

In May 1984, my Baseball coach asked me if I had ever called a softball game? I told him no, but he insisted that I could do it. When I got to the field, I saw two young ladies in dresses coaching the girls' softball team. With about five minutes left in the game, the 3rd base coach called time out, came down, and started an argument with me? She stated that the other team was batting out of order! She then asked me what I was going to do about it? I told her they were winning by 12 runs, and with only five minutes left, it did not matter!

She said I was supposed to call them out for batting out of turn! I told her to go back to her coaching box so this game could be over! When the game was over, she asked if I was going to call any more of their games, and I told her NO! She said good, because they had a game the next day! I stated that I had to sing at Church tomorrow night, so I was sure I would not be there!

As fate would have it, I was asked to call their game the next night! At the end of the game, she came down and said we thought you had to sing tonight at Church because we were going to come and hear you! I gave them the address to the Church, and they showed up as Church was ending! We went out to dinner afterward, and a year later, Regina and I were married!

Meeting Regina on that Baseball field changed my life forever and helped me to become the Man I am today! We have been married for 38 years with two sons and four grandchildren! Baseball has been very good to me!

I had no desire to stay at Kroger long, but I went into the management program four years later. I was able to use all the skills I learned working on the farm!

I became a store Manager and have run 9 different stores over the years. I opened 2 new stores and built some incredible teams that broke Sales Records in virtually every store! While I never made it to the big leagues in baseball, I have had the opportunity to make a difference in the lives of the many people and communities I have served. I was eventually moved into the Corporate Office as Customer Service Manager for the Atlanta Division. I did not make it is a Sportscaster, but I am on the Microphone at Kroger for every event that we have!

I will never forget what my Father taught me, which helped me transform from a boy to a man! I am still singing every chance that I get! The Bible says that your gift will make room for You! The gift that my Father taught me has lasted for a lifetime! I am still working for Kroger 43 years later, and I know this is where my life was designed to be.

Someone once said: "If you desire to be great, you must be willing to serve"! That is what my Father showed me as he served our Family, the Church, and the Communities where we lived. His legacy will forever live on because He taught me, *"Johnny, sometimes You just have to <u>Hope</u> them out!"*

About Johnny

Johnny Brown is a Native of Georgia and has lived there all his life! Johnny's lived in rural Hancock County and developed his work ethic while doing jobs on His Cousin's farm in Sparta Ga. His desire to play Professional Baseball landed him a scholarship to attend Clark College in 1976 to play baseball. Johnny majored in Mass Communications with a concentration in Broadcast Management!

Brown graduated in 1880 after being named MVP in both 1979 and 1980 and waited for the Scouts to come calling! Johnny started playing Semi-Pro Baseball and landed a job at Kroger part-time at the Disco Kroger in Buckhead! Even though Johnny had no desire to stay at Kroger, He found himself still there after 9 years and decided to enter the Management Program.

Brown excelled and went on to Manage 10 different stores before being promoted to Kroger Personal Finance Manager for the Atlanta Division! Johnny has been at Kroger for 43 years and received numerous awards for community service including:

The Barney Kroger National Community Service Award, The Kraft National Community Service Award, The Atlanta Mayor's Community Service Award and most recently, The Georgia Minority Business Award for Distinguished Service!

Johnny has been married to Regina Beal Brown for 38 years! They have 2 son's Jeremy and Timothy, and Daughter In Law Deanna and 3 beautiful Grandkids, Dawn, Jason and Jacob! Johnny lives by the Motto: "People don't care how much You know, until they know how much You care!"

Maine Man

MARVIS COX

There were many nights that passed in my home as a child without food, but my family and I found comfort in each other's presence. As a five-year-old, I would rush to every window, watching my mother's every step as she left for her 16 to 18-hour night shifts. It pained me to know that she had to rely on public transportation, especially late at night when the streets were filled with weirdos and creeps. I vividly remember one man dressed in a long brown coat who would follow my mother to the bus stop and expose himself to her.

The situation escalated to the point where he even appeared outside our apartment window, shamelessly flaunting his nakedness. However, one fateful day, my mother, cousin, brother, and I were heading to the store when we noticed this man standing outside our apartment. Without hesitation, my mother and cousin confronted him, causing him to feel embarrassed and fearful. He attempted to escape, but my cousin skillfully drove alongside him while my brother and I screamed, "Stay away from our mom!"

My mother and cousin unleashed a bunch of words I had never heard before, ensuring we never saw that man again. At that moment, it felt like a victory, but the harsh reality remained. Despite the triumph, my mother still had to walk down that same street the next day because we didn't have a car. I wished I were older and stronger to protect her, but I wasn't there yet. As I heard the faint voices of my three-year-old brother saying he was hungry, I realized that we had run out of snacks to sustain us through the night. We had no leftovers, and whatever we ate had to be made from scratch. It was just my brother and me at home, as our father was absent, leaving a void I had to fill.

Growing up, I had never been allowed in the kitchen while the adults were cooking. All I knew about cooking was a memory of watching my uncle over the stove late at night, twirling a pickle jar over the fire, and adding ice. With no other option, I climbed onto the kitchen counter and searched the cabinets for something to cook with. All I found was a steel salad bowl. There were only two eggs in the fridge, so I decided to give it a try.

I turned on the stove, not knowing any better, and placed the steel bowl on it without using any oil. The bowl turned black, but I went ahead and cracked the eggs into it, hoping for a different outcome. The smell that filled the air was unbearable, and I had no choice but to shut off the stove. It was a complete failure on my part, but my brother reassured me, saying it was okay and that I had tried my best.

Another night passed in hunger, and I found myself standing on the counter next to the sink, biting my nails and searching the dark skies for answers to our problems. But there was only stillness in the sky and dark clouds. It was at that moment that I realized I needed to set aside my childish desires and step up to take care of my family. As we grew older, I became better at cooking, and I gained a reputation as the king of making ham and cheese sandwiches.

One day, when my mother came home from work, exhausted and in need of replenishment, I had a sandwich and some chips waiting for her. When she first saw the food on the table, she laughed and asked who it was for. I proudly replied, "It's for you, Momma." She squinted her eyes and asked if I had washed my hands before making the food. We both laughed, and I assured her that I had.

She took a bite and then said something that filled me with pride. She said, "From now on, your nickname will be Maine Man." Confused, I asked her what that meant. She explained that it meant I was her main man, the man of the house. It was a moment of accomplishment and validation for me. From that point on, I took it upon myself to take care of everything around the house, from cleaning to cooking and helping my brother with his homework. However, as I entered high school, managing everything became increasingly challenging. I was involved in every sport imaginable, working a job and trying to balance my responsibilities at home.

On top of that, I now had a girlfriend. Juggling all these commitments became chaotic, and I started to feel overwhelmed. The stress began to take its toll, and I found myself getting into fights at school. This behavior was not conducive to my success, and I was eventually expelled. My mother had reached her breaking point with constantly transferring me to different schools, and she made it clear that I was on my own if I got kicked out again. I understood her frustration but didn't expect her to stop helping me altogether.

It's hard to believe that I'm almost at the finish line of graduation when I suddenly find myself in a major fight at school. As a result, I'm immediately kicked out, leaving me with only five months to graduate high school on time. If I don't, I'll be held back a grade. This news couldn't have come at a worse time because my girlfriend just told me she was pregnant. I felt like my back was against the wall. How could I take care of both my girlfriend and a baby while working a low-paying job and without a proper education? Feeling desperate, I turned to my mom for help, but she looked at me with no expression on her face. Then, she delivers the hard truth. She tells me that from this point on, my future will be determined by the choices I make. Unfortunately, she won't be able to assist me anymore. I'm dumbfounded and struggle to comprehend what she means. But soon enough, reality hits me harder than ever before. This is the moment of my transition into manhood.

It's time to face the harsh truths about life. I realized that nobody could answer my questions except for God, and the chapters of my life are just beginning. I had to decide when and what to do with the rest of my life. I had to rely on my faith in God to guide me through it all. I took matters into my own hands and enrolled myself in a new school, determined to finish without any help from my mother. I wanted to prove to her and everyone else that I am a man who stands on his own two feet, not someone who relies on others.

I researched high schools in my area and discovered that only one school would accept me. I attended orientation, selected my classes, and figured out the best plan to graduate on time. Despite the school's rough neighborhood and distractions, I made a firm decision to graduate on time, and I stuck to it. I took everything seriously. I attended every tutoring session available for the classes I struggled with. I refrained from hanging out with anyone at the school or engaging in conversations that didn't benefit my grades.

I stayed out of trouble and kept my eyes on the prize. When graduation day arrived, only thirty-four students out of a hundred and nine walked across the stage. I am proud to say that I am one of those thirty-four. With high school behind me, it was time to pick up the pace. My girlfriend had just given birth to our baby boy. This new responsibility lit a fire within me. I am determined to be better than my father. I found myself working three jobs and juggling college at the same time.

One cold night while working at the airport, something dawned on me. It's as if God is telling me that it's time for something new. That night, as my co-workers and I rode along in the airport shuttle bus, the lack of heat and freezing wind made me complain about the cold. An older man in the back speaks up, reminding me that if I can't handle a little cold, I won't be able to handle the challenges of the military. This remark sparks a heated argument between us. I believe I can handle anything and that there's no challenge I can't conquer. So, in response to the man's challenge, I decided to go to the recruiter's office the next day. And just like that, God answers the call to bring me into manhood with authority, honor, and determination. Through this experience of working side by side with the men in the military, I was taught that not all disagreements require physical confrontation to solve. I now understand that I must walk the path set by God's vision, fill the shoes that were never designed, and conquer the space given to me on Earth while seeking answers to life's hard truths.

I finally understood that I need to live my life in God's image, be slow to anger, lean towards loving others, and forgive those who may not know any better. Thank you, Lord, for guiding me in my journey. I saw then, but I see even better now, that from a young boy until now, you were not only preparing me to be any man but a TRUE MAN OF GOD. The challenges I have overcome in my life were all by your mercy and grace. You are the reason I am proud to say I am not just a man, I'M THE MAINE MAN.

About Marvis

Marvis F. Cox Sr. is a decorated War Hero and Veteran, born in Chicago, Illinois in the winter of 1981. He served in the United States Army Infantry, attaining the rank of E5 Sergeant. In 2001, Marvis joined the Army and was deployed to Iraq as part of Operation Iraqi Freedom in response to the events of 9/11. Over the course of 9 years, he completed three deployments overseas before being honorably discharged due to service-connected disabilities from the war.

After his military service, Marvis pursued his passion for education and graduated from Waubonsee College in 2015 with a dual Degree in the arts. He continued to explore his interests, including welding and truck driving, obtaining his CDL. However, it was his love for writing that ultimately led him to embark on a new journey as an author and entrepreneur.

Marvis is currently a co-founder and branding consultant for YoungSavedLeaders/ClassEDefined LLC. He is a proud member of the ForbesBlk Community and actively advocates for Lupus and Thyroid Cancer Awareness, supporting his wife Jacquiline in her fight against these conditions. Additionally, he is passionate about advocating for children with ADHD and Autism.

As a Life Coach for urban and troubled youth, Marvis utilizes his personal experiences to inspire and motivate others. He is also a sought-after Motivational Speaker, sharing his story of resilience and determination. In his ongoing commitment to his community, Marvis plans to open his own nonprofit organization, providing troubled youth with a safe space to learn discipline and leadership skills, regardless of the challenges they face in their environment.

Marvis has already made significant contributions to the literary world. He is the author of "My Box of Chocolates" and a co-author in an anthology titled "Unknown Battlefields". Additionally, he is collaborating with his youngest son on an upcoming project called "My Superpowers are Not Weird", which focuses on children who struggle with acceptance due to their autistic traits.

Outside of his professional endeavors, Marvis takes immense pride in being a loving father to his five children and one puppy. He currently resides in Illinois with his children and his wife Jacquiline.

Through his writing, advocacy work, and dedication to empowering others, Marvis F. Cox Sr. continues to make a positive impact on the world around him.

The Man Who Was Hardly A Boy

BRANDON DORRINGTON

At the end of my third-grade school year during the early 1990's while in Michigan , Mom told me that it was time for her to now withhold any emotional support toward me and that from that day forth I should only expect a roof over my head, clothes on my back, and rice, butter, and sugar in my stomach. I consciously understood that I was, at that moment in time, crossing some sort of threshold, and my life was now going to drastically change direction. The path ahead was destined to be lonely, but it was ultimately my choice to decide my fate.

My first ever life-threatening crisis occurred when I was in fifth grade, lying in my bed at home on a school night. While contemplating the traumatic events that had happened over the previous two years, I began looking around my room and witnessed for myself that I was physically, as well as emotionally, alone. In that moment, I finally realized how serious my situation was as the following facts became clear: my parents are divorced, my sister is dead, and all my other brothers and sisters live with my dad, and now I'm the only one getting whipped by Mom after she tells me how much I look like my father. Mom moved away from Kalamazoo, from everybody after our family was broken, so now it's just me and her in a distant town; stranded, bankrupt, and without a pot to piss in or a window to throw it out of.

Grandma, aunts, uncles, cousins, childhood friends and community members that I grew up with are now non-existent. My new next-door neighbor and my new friend's older brother got arrested for murder and armed robbery and were convicted and sentenced to life in prison without the possibility of parole. So now Mom tells me to come straight home from school, lock the door, and not go outside while she is hardly ever home due to working two jobs. After several months of this, I feel like I'm the one who's incarcerated, so I sneak out the window just to play outside like the rest of the kids. On top of this, I recently had to decide to either fight all my neighbors every day at school and after school or join the local gang.

With all these thoughts running through my mind, I had a hard time going to sleep. I couldn't help feeling like it would perhaps be better to give up the ghost and die at this point. Therefore, I could not prevent the out of body experience from happening, which almost killed me due to years of unnoticed and unrecognized trauma from this multitude of uncontrollable events. Moving forward I knew that the best way for me to survive and eventually escape my circumstances was with perseverance, relentless zeal, and returning fire with no mercy, because I was not granted mercy when I needed it the most. With this ideology, perspective, and enlightenment at ten years old, I didn't have the luxury of being a boy any longer.

I started seventh grade. On the first day of the school year, I became ecstatic during lunch time after witnessing the wide variety and multiple food options that were not available to me in elementary school. I immediately filled my tray with cookies, potato chips, juice boxes, French fries, and two cheeseburgers, only to get in line and reach the lunch lady and be told that my total amount due was $5.25. I told her that my name was on the free lunch list and that I did not need to pay anything. Due to my lack of knowledge about the situation, I found myself suspended from school with an additional two days of after school detention.

I only had the opportunity to visit my father four days per month, and I told him about the lunch incident because my mom had placed me on "punishment" right after it happened. After having that difficult conversation with my dad, he explained that he paid my mom child support every month, and I should ask her if I can do any extra chores or work around the apartment to earn a few bucks so I could buy snacks at school and avoid conflict and future disciplinary action. The time eventually came for me to muster up the courage to have this conversation with Mom. After I told her the plan that Dad and I came up with, all hell broke loose, and I was given a rude awakening. To say the least, the plan went all bad and the deal was completely off the table. Weeks, months, and years passed with me having absolutely no money or even the slightest chance in hell to earn any. So, I started thinking, and created my own earning methods outside of my mom's house. Just to say it nicely, I got paid on the block with no remorse and by any means necessary. This is what exposed me to the "dark side."

One week before my 17th birthday I decided that I had had enough of the abuse at home, the desperate measures taken for cash, and running from the cops. So, I took the initiative to return to my city of birth in hopes to reunite with distant relatives and possibly have a better life. Although, I had to leave Mom, my best friends, and everything that I had become accustomed to for the past 12 years behind, it was required for my survival. I had finally made it to my senior year of high school, and the thought of only having one year left until I'm completely on my own motivated me to create an exit strategy from my mother's house. I needed this plan to be flawless, perfect, and executed well in a limited amount of time, so I started meditating every day before and after school. I figured that if I could somehow run enough game and graduate high school, I would most definitely be a man then. However, after graduating from high school and then basic training in the Army, I still didn't quite feel like a man; just the same as before with no different, distinct internal change.

After the 9/11 attacks on New York City occurred I was on active duty in the military and I was determined to give the utmost service to my country in the highest regard, which would be to put my life on the line, so I volunteered to go fight the war on terror in Iraq. Eventually, I was deployed on two different occasions, first in 2003 and again in 2004. I returned home after being honorably discharged, and even though I had been to hell and back, I still didn't quite feel like a full-fledged man. Something seemed off, but I couldn't quite determine what that was or why. So, I sought out other opportunities to learn what it is to be a man and prove myself.

My next adventure was attending college. I enrolled in Dillard University, attended class, made the Dean's list, and even joined the honors program while studying under the most challenging tenured professors, including the future emeritus as his mentee for over a decade. However, I still thought that true manhood was outside of my grasp. During a conversation with my mentor about the importance of healthy relationships, I realized that my relationship with my biological father had been strained for over 30 years at that point. Not having that healthy relationship affected what manhood looked like for me, or – I thought – whether I would ever achieve it.

I did not have the slightest clue where to begin my next attempt to achieve manhood, so I ventured to serve my country in another capacity- I ran for mayor. Despite giving it my best effort and complete dedication, with a platform touting non-profit organization collaboration, youth mentorship, criminal justice reform, and economic development, I fell short in the race. I considered the loss as a failed mission on my quest to become a man, so I decided to pull myself up by my bootstraps, dust myself off, and re-calibrate collectively.

I then began a spiritual journey; leaving all my treasures, possessions, and everything of material value behind. As I moved forward and embraced the ideology to no longer care what others thought of me in any capacity, my burdens seemed just a little lighter. But after three years of traveling the East Coast, South, and Midwest – living from pillar to post, hand to mouth, and not knowing when or where I would be able to take a shower – things got stressful. Occasionally I would fast for a period of four days and nights, only drinking water.

Then I began "finding" money to go to the liquor store and purchase a fifth of gin and a pack of Kools or Newport shorts, depending on what part of the country I was in. Months passed as I continued drinking and smoking my pain, sorrow, and despair away. I thought it was a great coping mechanism. I admit that in some strange way it was enjoyable, however, after sobering up my problems were still there. That was the end of using that strategy.

At this point I desperately needed to make another move if I was going to survive this journey but I didn't know what the hell I was supposed to do because I had tried everything under the sun and nothing new was in sight. Upon waking up to another day after nearly having another out of body experience, I finally decided to just live one day at a time; no longer giving any thought whatsoever to yesterday or tomorrow and solely focusing on the present. My only plan in life was to eat, sleep, and sh$$; with no other agenda at hand. As the days, weeks and eventually months went by without talking to anyone, having minimal shelter, and little to no food, I began to observe everything around me – the birds, trees, people, and vehicles – while staring with a sharp gaze into space.

Listening to the wind blow, feeling the cold and warm air, and sinking my feet into Mother Earth, I felt absent from time. I was a ship with no water to sail in, a seed with no dirt to be planted in, a bag of Ramen noodles with no pot to cook in. Suddenly, things finally started to make sense; the notion of $2 + 2 = 4$ was reasonable and $a + b + c = d$ became rational and the internal along with the external aligned perfectly. Inductive and deductive reasoning was born, input equaled output, and analysis versus paralysis was starting to be measured.

Due to being blackballed from the New Orleans educational system I had to seek an alternative route to making money, so I returned to the racetrack, which is more dangerous than the St. Bernard housing projects. Work began at 4 AM, seven days per week. I learned to dread tomorrow because I knew the alarm clock was going to go off at 3:30 AM and I would be required to shovel horse sh$$, piss, and garbage for hours, and even walk four to five miles, all before 9 AM.

Regardless of the weather conditions, temperature and elements, the job needed to be done. I was homeless at this period in my life, so at night I found a place to sleep in the barn with the horses, goats, and chickens on hay and straw, but I didn't complain because after not having at least one day off in months, the dirt floor felt like a king size pediatric mattress from Rooms to Go. I managed to start saving money and eating a full entre of healthy food every day, which gave me something to thank the ancestors for despite all of the trials and tribulations that I continued to go through. So, after the sun set every day, I cleaned and shined my jungle boots and prepared for work the next day because I couldn't afford to get fired for lack of preparation or over sleeping and showing up to work one minute after 4 AM.

One day my phone rang, and I heard my father's voice on the other end, "Son how are you doing?" He told me that one of the brothers from my childhood church home had a job opportunity available in Michigan. I was excited, but if I were able to set up an interview, I would be absent from work, which would get me fired. Therefore, I desperately needed to ensure that I secured that job if I traveled there, because I was at the point of no return. That night, I began thinking about my current brutal life of exhaustion, physical fatigue, and long suffering. However, as nice as those variables would be to delete, at that time in my life a job was a job and bread needed to be put on the table. With no feelings or emotions involved, I reached a conclusion based on choosing the best option available to me in a capitalist society. My next move had to be my best move, so I planned my escape from my life of pain for the day after my next payday.

When that day came, I packed my duffle bags at 4 AM. I had one last thought about staying at the racetrack but said, "F@$% it. I'm out," and I drove away. After arriving in Michigan, I met my father for breakfast at a famous local restaurant. While we were eating, Dad got a call from the brother about the job and was informed that the position had already been filled. "Damn it!" I said, "It was all good a week ago!" I thought that I had f@$%ed up. But my dad said, "Don't worry, I was going to remodel my basement all by myself, but if you are willing to help me, I will pay you."

The thought of my dad paying me seemed like a good faith effort, however, I also considered the fact that this would be a once in a lifetime opportunity for us to rebuild our relationship. So, I spent the next 18 months with my father, consciously making the effort to see my dad every day since I was 5 years old. I began to learn his ways, hear all his stories, and see what it was like walking in his shoes while repairing the father-son bond that was broken almost 33 years ago. During this course of time, I asked my father the million-dollar question, "Dad, can you please teach me how to be a man?"

"Yes, Son," he replied. And the rest is history.

About Brandon

Brandon Dorrington is an Advisory Council Member at Bastion Community of Resilience.

He has a Master of Arts in Criminal Justice and currently resides in New Orleans, LA.,

Brandon's skills include documentaries and research writing (Veterans Journey Home and Positivist vs Classical School of Thought.

Brandon enjoys fasting, mountain climbing and rifling.

"Character Matters"

Donald Davis

As I look back over my journey from boyhood to manhood, I ask myself *Why was I born? Why am I here? What is my purpose?* These questions, if only for a moment during times of reflection, come to mind every so often. Even more so now that I am retired and seem to have more time on my hands. I ask myself *Has mine been a life well lived?* As I reflect upon those thoughts, the lessons learned, the things I've seen, and the experiences I've had, one word keeps coming to mind – service.

I've always felt the greatest joy and satisfaction when I was serving others. Whether it was as a young man taking care of my brother and sisters, serving in the military taking care of my soldiers, or taking care of my employees and customers for many years after the military, or, most importantly, taking care of my wife and son during all of those years, it was done with great joy because it was in the service of others. It was never about me. Doing what I can, no matter how small, to make the life of another person better, makes a difference.

I was the first born of my generation into a large family. I did not have my father in my life, but I had many aunts and uncles who made it possible for me not to miss that one important part of my development. They all seemed to go the extra mile to ensure I received the attention, love, and direction I needed to grow into the person I was to become. At an early age, they treated me as though I was one of them – an adult, not a child. For that reason, I did not miss having my biological father in my life.

From the time I was old enough to understand, my family was teaching me. My aunts taught me how to cook, clean the house, wash and iron clothes for the week, even braid my sisters' hair. I learned everything related to taking care of a home and a family. I was a natural, and I seemed to enjoy doing it. I once asked my mother why I needed to learn these things. Her response was, "You're good at it, and we don't want you to depend on others to do things for you."

Little did I know, they were preparing me for a life of service to others. And I *was* good at it – doing for others and not expecting anything in return. When I was growing up in the 1960s and early 1970s, the focus was on the family. We did not have the technology we have today, or in some cases, the distractions, as I sometimes say. The focus was on teaching kids what mattered most: having structure; discipline; hard work; caring for others; being the best you; and doing the right thing because it was the right thing to do. I gained appreciation for these values while sitting at the feet of my grandmother as she would work on a quilt, listening to her stories of old and her dreams of a future for me. Life was simple, and I felt as if anything was possible.

As a teenager, I was a straight A student. I enjoyed sports and school in general because it came so easy for me. Math was my favorite subject; so much so that I wanted to become a math teacher. I thought I had my future all planned out-graduate high school, go to college, become a teacher then get married and start my own family. But sometimes the plans we envision for ourselves don't work out as intended. However, if we embrace every opportunity, we can accomplish anything.

As I grew older, I was included more and more in the adult conversations within my family. It may have been because I was the oldest in my generation, or the fact I did not know my biological father. I never met my biological father, the times when I would ask my mother about my father she would get very angry. I wanted to know what he was like, was I like him, I still wonder to this day. Regardless, it was not until then that I realized there was a lot for me to learn and experience out in the world. I wanted to continue to grow and thought being out in the world was the way to do it. The foundation was set, and being exposed to different cultures and the opportunities to meet people from different backgrounds is what helped shape me. It opened my eyes to the possibilities.

All of my uncles served in either the Army or the Air Force. Back then, if you wanted a future, the military was the way to go. When they would come home on leave, seeing them in uniform was awe inspiring. I always felt as if they were coming home just to see me. My uncles spending time with me, wanting to know how I was doing, and sharing their travels and experiences with me made me feel like I was special to them. Listening to their stories inspired my dream to enter the military and travel the world – exploring new cultures and meeting people from different backgrounds. Seeing people in other parts of the world who didn't have much in the material sense yet were full of joy and willing to share what they did have, showed me what life was all about. That experience is what helped shape me into the person I am today.

When the time came for me to step out on my own, I was unaware that my true identity had already been formed by the way my family cared for me. I was smart, confident, disciplined, and most importantly, kind. Caring for others came naturally; I did not think about it, it just happened. I knew who I was, and I was determined to stay true to being that person no matter what. There were times and situations when doing the right thing was tested. I was always taught and believe that you treat people the way you want to be treated, no matter what. During my military career I learned you lead by example. In 2010 as a store manager for the Kroger company I was responsible for 120 employees. I was instructed by my district manager to fire my grocery manager because he did not like him, not because of job performance but for personal reasons. I refused because it was the wrong thing to do. Mistreating people is not who I am. I stood on principle and after our conversation my district manager agreed. My character matters.

Going along to get along for personal gain seemed to be the norm, but deep down I knew it was wrong. Making the right decision may have cost me in the short term, but as I look back, in the long run it was the right thing to do. I've been abundantly blessed because of it.

Back when I was still dating my wife of almost 40 years, she would often tell me, "You're a people person; people are just drawn to you."

Not thinking about it, I would respond, "That's just who I am."

People can tell if you're sincere in the things you say and do. It matters because you never know who's watching you. You may never know the impact you have just by what you say or do, no matter how small it may be.

I remember two such encounters.

In 2010 while working for the Kroger company l was the store manager for a large grocery store in Powder Springs, Georgia. I was sent to this store to build a team of associates to better serve the local community. I had a way of getting people to do what needed to be done in order to accomplish whatever the task was. By leadership within the company I was a very inclusive manger. The people who worked for me knew I cared about them as a person. Building trust and being the same person every day, (willing to teach, train, coach, praise for a job well done). I enjoyed helping people be there best and do their best work.

My district operations manager sent a young man named Robert to work in my meat department as a meat clerk. He had worked in several different stores and had difficulty getting along with other associates and sometimes serving our customers. Robert was in his early twenties, very smart but needed work on his people skills. He just needed to feel like he was a part of the team. As for our store, I was the example. Everyone was following my lead. I treated all associates the same, they trusted me and would follow my instructions because they knew what role they had in accomplishing the company goals in serving our customer I was told Robert was troubled, and if anyone could do something with him Mr. Davis could. When he came into my office, I explained to him that he was now a part of my store family, what my expectations of him were and what he could expect from me.

As time went on, I had some problems with this young man, but I was determined not to give up on him. Robert would have trouble interacting with other associates within the meat department. He seemed to think he was always being attacked, he was very defensive of his actions even when he was wrong. I would counsel and encourage him. Praise him when he did well and coach him when he needed it. He began to see that Mr. Davis was a man of his word and cared about him succeeding. Then one day he came to me and asked, "Mr. Davis, why have you been so nice to me when I have been such an ass?"

He had been watching me, and thought he knew how I would respond to him based on his prior experiences. I didn't follow the script he was familiar with, so he wanted to know what was different. At first, I was taken aback by his question. I thought about it for a few seconds and explained again that he was a part of my team, and this is how we do things.

He asked his question again. He still did not understand. So, I informed him that, at the end of the day, it does not matter how you treat me, what matters to me is how I treat you. I'm not responsible for you, I'm responsible for me. From that point on he was a changed person – happy, outgoing, and very engaged in doing his best every day. He knew I truly cared about him as a person, not just as an employee. _He went on to become a manager of his own meat department. He would stop in to see me, ask questions about the department and tell me how great it was having his own department. For me, that's having an impact as a man; being that example in both word and deed. Was this a chance encounter? I dare say, not. It was an opportunity to reaffirm my identity – who I am as a man.

In another encounter, another young man who worked for me said, "Mr. Davis, one day I want to be just like you." Damian was nineteen years old and worked in my Deli department. He was great with customers, friendly and always had a big smile. You could not walked by him without stopping for a quick conversation.

I replied, "I don't want you to be like me."

From the look on his face, you would have thought that I ruined his day. I informed him that I wanted him to be *better* than me. I told him he could be anything he wanted to be. That he has opportunities I didn't have. So, I asked him, "Now what do you want to do? Who do you want to be?"

He could not answer that question. So, I told him, "When you decide, you let me know."

As time went on, I forgot about that conversation, but apparently it had been on his mind. Sometime later he came to me and said, "Mr. Davis, I know what I want to do. I want to go to school for air conditioning and refrigeration." Damian had been working for me about six months. It was about two months after our conversation that he had decided what he wanted to do. This was in 2013 and in early 2014 he left to attend school for air conditioning and refrigeration.

I asked him why and how that became his choice. He told me that his uncle was in that line of work, and that when he was little, his uncle would take him on jobs with him. His uncle enjoyed his work and he enjoyed being with him. Listening to the young man's stories, learning about the work his uncle was doing, and seeing the excitement on his face as he relayed these accounts was really something special. His uncle had a big impact on his life. He just needed to be reminded of that. He may not have revisited his time with his uncle if I had not taken the time to encourage him- just by being approachable and kind in my interactions with him as a person and not just as my employee. He did go back to school and is now doing very well as a heating and air conditioning technician.

By just going about my day, unaware that I was being watched, reaffirmed that you can be a positive influence and not even know it. Taking the time to interact with someone on a personal level can have a profound impact on the course of their life. It's a wonderful feeling when they come back and say, "You made a difference in my life."

As we journey through life, the experiences and challenges we face help to define the impact we will have on those we may come into contact with, and we should choose to have a positive impact. Always be mindful that you can be a difference maker.

There are many twists and turns on the road from boyhood to manhood, and that's what's so exciting. There are opportunities to choose to do the right thing because it's the right thing to do or go along to get along. If you go along just to get along, think about the missed opportunities to have a positive impact in the life of another and the blessings that come along with it. So, choose to do the right thing.

Along this journey, I have learned that a life well lived is a life of service and compassion for others. For me, being a man of integrity who will always strive to do the right thing is the legacy I want to leave.

About Donald

Donald Davis retired from the United States Army after serving twenty-one years which ten of those years were spent in Germany. That allowed Donald to travel throughout Europe, experiencing the culture and meeting people from diverse backgrounds.

Upon retirement, Donald moved to Marietta, Georgia with his wife and son and went to work for a major retailer as a store manager and over twenty-four years managed stores throughout the metro Atlanta area.

Donald's unique ability to connect with people and inspire people allowed him to have a life-changing impact on everyone he came into contact with. Donald retired again in early 2023 and continues to inspire those he comes into contact with.

Donald attends church regularly and is actively involved in the men's ministry at First Baptist Church Atlanta, he enjoys reading, traveling, and attending car shows. You can contact Donald at Davisdonald6@AOL.com.

Advice To My Younger Self

KEVIN EASTMAN

Oh, Man! If I could go back and sit down with younger Kevin and have a heart-to-heart conversation with him! The accomplishments I'd tell him that he's going to see from himself would absolutely blow his mind. The only problem is that depending on what age I would have caught him to have that conversation, he wouldn't believe much of what I told him. Why wouldn't he? Like most young adolescents, it's because he is extremely hard-headed and fallaciously thinks he knows everything.

Let me explain that.

I was born and raised in Oakland, California. If you know anything about Oakland's history, you know that during the

1970s, it was predominantly a proud, blue-collar city with hard-working people who cared about their respective communities. However, it had a hard-nosed reputation. Even Oakland's professional sports teams, the Raiders and Athletics, personified toughness. The Black Panther Party was also a prominent main staple in Oakland. There were (and still are) areas of Oakland where there is one way in, and one way out, so you had to pay attention to where you were going, because it is easy to get caught in the wrong part of the city.

Despite Oakland's rough exterior appearance and rough reputation, the goal, at least in the 1970s, for many parents and grandparents was to set the next generations up for success. They used their personal experiences and historical knowledge to pour what they could into my generation.

I can remember listening to endless, gripping stories of courage and triumph of people who looked like me, who constantly faced adversity and overcame it. This was while being surrounded by images portrayed on television of people of color being portrayed on many popular 70s sitcoms (which I love, by the way) as service industry workers, junk dealers, street hustlers, winos, and domestic workers. This created a conflict in my mind because while I was being told by many people that I could do anything I set my mind to, I was being shown images that didn't quite coincide with the picture they were painting.

It wasn't until a sitcom featuring a black man who owned his own dry-cleaning business premiered that the idea of the possibility of success started to take shape for me. Before that, success beyond working full-time, 9 to 5, seemed like a rarity—a unicorn of sorts. It was something you'd heard about, but no one around you every day ever really achieved it. I guess it would also depend on your definition of success.

During the 1980s, I saw more people become what most would generally consider "successful," but unfortunately, many of those people achieved that success through illegal activity. A not-so-small number of people I saw become successful was due to drug dealing. They had money, houses, cars, women, entourages, and clothes – everything an impressionable mid-to-late teenager needed to see. It was a fast, easy way to escape "living in the hood."

Keep in mind that at the same time, I was seeing those real-life images of people my age with all their perceived success, I was being coached by the influencers I had, who were still in my ear, telling me I could do anything I set my mind to and to remain on the straight and narrow. Truthfully speaking, staying on the straight and narrow wasn't a hard choice for me, thanks to an extremely traumatic event I experienced years earlier.

I was in the 7th grade, and one day at lunchtime, a friend I'd known since the third grade asked me to skip school with him. I refused because I was afraid of getting caught. I knew I didn't want to deal with my parents if I had been caught skipping school. I decided to stay at school because dealing with my friends would be easier than dealing with my parents. Little did I know that in less than 24 hours, my world would be flipped on its ear.

The next day, I learned that my friend I'd known since the third grade, never made it home. There was an unfortunate accident, and he'd lost his life. Few things can drive home the message of how fast life can come at you more emphatically than seeing your friend lying in a casket, knowing you were just talking to him days earlier, and mere hours before he died. I couldn't help but wonder what could have happened if I'd gone with him. It could have easily been *me* lying in that casket. So, that took care of any thoughts I had of straying from the straight and narrow path. For me, the alternative was listening to the people who were trying to teach me other life lessons.

It wasn't always easy to listen to their stories. Some of those lessons required a lot of sacrifice, which was more than I was willing to pay in my limited capacity at the time. What they did succeed at was planting the seed. What my life experiences did was to provide water.

So, eventually, I developed the desire to go somewhere away from Oakland. It wasn't a bad place, at least from my standpoint, but my influencers' words had hit their mark. I knew there was more to the world than Oakland, and I was determined to discover it as much as I could. Joining the Air Force seemed like the easiest way to do that, so that's exactly what I did.

What initially was a plan to serve four years turned into a career of twenty years. Throughout that time, I learned many more lessons than the ones I was taught prior. In the Air Force, I had to confront overt racism, only to be basically blown off. I had nay-sayers trying to stop me from pursuing various goals I was trying to set for myself. In fact, the only goal they all encouraged was to further my education.

In addition, I had to deal with sabotage—meaning navigating around people trying to impede my progress. You know, it's interesting: you'd think people on your team would be rooting for you because the team exceeds if all the members do. However, some people feel they need to hold *you* back for *them* to progress, probably out of fear that you will pass them.

During my time in the Air Force, I was fortunate enough to run into some wonderful mentors who cared about my development and guided me in a positive direction. My mentors in Oakland may have laid the foundation, but my Air Force mentors built the rest of the house... sometimes by force.

The achievements I obtained in the Air Force are numerous. College? Done. Three times, in fact. Promotions? I earned every one of them. Individual and team performance awards? Multiple times. I was selected to work in two of the most misunderstood career fields: Military Training Instructor and Recruiter. Each time, I had people trying to discourage me. Had I listened to them, I wouldn't have enjoyed the Air Force as much as I did. Not bad for a kid from the inner city of Oakland, huh?

What is my intent? I'd like to share some valuable life lessons I've learned along the way. Many of those lessons taught to me as a boy have helped shape the man I am today. Hopefully, one or two of these lessons will inspire some other young person to choose a different path before it's too late for them to make an adjustment. Just think about my boy. When he woke up that fateful morning, and even during the conversation we had during lunch that day, I couldn't imagine that dying was on his list of things to do.

Lesson 1: You will never succeed at anything as long as you are afraid to fail. Failure is an important part of the path to success. You must fail in order to succeed, because lessons aren't learned when things go right—they're learned when things go *wrong*! The difference between stagnation and progress is the application of the lessons taught by those things going wrong.

What am I trying to say? You must respect yourself enough to know when you need help to get you to the next step and be wise enough to not let your ego stand in the way of getting that help. Stubbornness can be costly. There's an old saying that goes, "If you think education is expensive, wait until you get the bill for being stupid."

Lesson 2: You can choose to let your situation, circumstances, or environment define you, or you can write your own definition by using those things as tools instead of a crutch or excuse. You can make these things work to your advantage or allow them to consume you, but you are in control of the decision. Just because you were born into a certain environment, it doesn't mean you must remain in it for the rest of your life. The entire world is out there, waiting for you to discover how you can fit into it. You need the motivation, a plan to get you there, and the will to execute the plan without the fear of failing. Failure isn't the end until you *make it* to the end.

I truly believe all of us were created for a purpose, and there is a reason you're reading this piece right now. Being born with "one strike" (as many of us were) doesn't mean you're already out. You still have two more strikes to go. What you must learn is to adjust your focus. See the pitch coming slower, and you can adjust your swing accordingly. Remember, it's easier to see a change-up coming at you than a fastball.

Mentors can make all the difference in your life. Who would have given a kid from the hood of Oakland a chance to do the things I've done? I never settled for less. I aimed for the highest point I could. I joined the Air Force (only four people from my graduating class did that), achieved three levels of higher education, got promoted six times, traveled to locations I never thought I'd see in person, and led the #1 recruiting team in the country in back-to-back years, and a top-10 recruiting team over 6 straight years. Those and other accomplishments were thanks in no small part to each mentor I had, in *and* out of the Air Force. Each of them invested in me, and now, I'm doing my best to live up to those investments by paying it forward to help others, much in the same manner that I was helped.

One fantastic philosophy I want to share with you is this gem I learned from one of many mentors: *"Do what's hard, when it's easy."* If you do hard things when they're easy, you can control the speed at which you have to deal with them. It's like driving a car or riding a bike. The faster you go, the less time you'll have to react.

Lastly, don't underestimate the importance of finding and having mentors. They worked wonders in my life. It's important to remember that mentees pick the mentor – not the other way around. So, use my experiences, make your own plan, and make your unique positive mark on society. There's enough success in the reserve tanks for everyone to have a slice, and there'd still be *plenty* left over!

Young Kevin wouldn't have believed what I told him had we sat down and talked back then. Many of the things he would have heard from me seemed impossible to him, given where he was. However, the desire to do something different (and probably better) was always in his mind, and that was the key to him opening up to those many mentors and receiving the information they offered him. As it turned out, he learned that the impossible is possible when you're willing to go after it. The rewards were well worth sacrifices, and he knew that he could accomplish any goal he set for himself and that the world was much bigger than Oakland, California.

About Kevin

Kevin is a native of Oakland, California, but currently resides in Riverside County, in Southern California. A skilled speaker and business management consultant with a passion for assisting others in achieving their goals, he thrives on simplicity and logic.

A graduate of Castlemont High School, he retired from active duty in the U.S. Air Force with over 20 years of service, in locations around the world, including San Antonio, Texas, Chicago, Illinois, Belize, South Korea, and Japan.

He served stints as a military training instructor (commonly known as a "drill" instructor), and over a decade as a recruiter at the high school, college, and post-graduate levels.

Kevin earned undergraduate degrees Human Resource Management, and Marketing, from the Community College of the Air Force and Columbia Southern University, respectively, as well as a graduate degree in Business Management, Marketing from Azusa Pacific University. He also holds certifications in Marketing, Professional Selling Skills, and Sales Coaching.

With the release of his debut book, *"Don't Gamble on Life Improvement... Until You Shift the Odds!"* he became a published author.

He is an active member of Alpha Phi Alpha Fraternity, Inc., an avid sports fan, and enjoys cooking, writing, meeting people, listening to music, watching movies, mentoring, traveling, and spending time with family and friends.

The Worst Day of My Life: The Beginning of a Changed Heart

HENRY EBERHART

March 17, 1988, I woke up with a hangover thinking I was coming out of a dream. The truth is, I was in the Fulton County jail after a jury trial that lasted a day and a half and I was found guilty.

The trial started on Monday. By midday I knew I would be found guilty, after all I really was guilty.

On day two, the case was given to the jury before lunch, instead of getting lunch I went to the liquor store and bought a pint of Scotch. By the time lunch was over the verdict was in, and I was found guilty and was on my way to Rice Street, the Fulton County jail.

I woke up on the morning of March 17th with a hangover and with no hope and no help. I had come to the end of myself with nowhere to turn. It was then I began to look back over my life, to take self-inventory.

There is a saying that goes, "you either get bitter or better!" I was determined that I would come out of this a better person. On March 27th, I gave my life to the Lord and Savior Jesus Christ.

So, here I am, 32 years old and incarcerated with a wife who is still grieving from the loss of a son who died less than six months earlier. She has not only lost a son but a husband too.

When I began to think about her, and all the mistakes I had made, not just in our marriage, but in life in general, I realized it was not my environment. It was not so much a lack of opportunity either. You see, my choices, bad decisions, and my cold heart led me to the Fulton County jail and ultimately to prison.

So, there I was in jail awaiting to be sentenced and potentially serving 20 years for aggravated assault knowing my life would be changed forever. With nowhere to turn I was finally at the end of my rope. The only place I knew to turn to was the Lord himself.

I remembered when I was first arrested my cousin Phyllis gave me a Bible and told me to read Acts 16, where Paul and Silas were in prison and their chains were miraculously released. I hoped to be released too. But God had other plans. I began to read my Bible not understanding most of it. One of the smallest, meanest, angriest men in a cell that was designed for 16 men which now held 34, came to me and asked if I understood what I was reading. I told him no, and he started asking me questions and to my surprise I had answers; then my eyes became open. The more I read the more I understood. To this day, I do not know if I was more surprised by the person asking me questions or my being able to answer questions. The more I understood the more I realized my heart was changing.

Eventually, I was transferred to Jackson Diagnostic and then to Rogers Correctional in Reidsville Georgia in August of 1988.

One evening I called my wife Molley and what happened next changed my whole perspective on life.

She asked me, "Why did I do the things I did to her?" I was so stunned I had no answers, I could not talk. I told her I would call her back. On the way back to the dormitory my thoughts were; this is probably the last time I would speak to her and maybe never see her again. Who could blame her based on all I had done. You see, for the first time I was afraid of losing my wife. Imagine that, I was not worried when I was right there in the home; but now that I am in prison, I am worried.

Once back in the dormitory, I asked the Lord to help me give her some answers. The Lord gave me much more than I asked for. Remember earlier I mentioned taking self-inventory? This is what the Lord gave me to start me on my journey of a changed heart.

Romans 1:16-22 NKJV

16 For I am not ashamed of the gospel of Christ, for it is the power of God to salvation for everyone who believes, for the Jew first and also for the Greek.

17 For in it the righteousness of God is revealed from faith to faith; as it is written, "The just shall live by faith."

18 For the wrath of God is revealed from heaven against all ungodliness and unrighteousness of men, who suppress the truth in unrighteousness,

19 because what may be known of God is manifest in them, for God has shown it to them.

20 For since the creation of the world His invisible attributes are clearly seen, being understood by the things that are made, even His eternal power and Godhead, so that they are without excuse,

21 because, although they knew God, they did not glorify Him as God, nor were thankful, but became futile in their thoughts, and their foolish hearts were darkened.

22 Professing to be wise, they became fools

Several thoughts pierced my mind immediately. God's salvation is available for me. To be justified in God's sight I must live faithfully. I was living an ungodly life. I knew of God, yet I was unthankful. Lastly, and obviously, I was a fool.

After realizing all of this, I began to take serious inventory of myself. The Lord gave the answer for my wife Molley. I wrote a 16-page letter front and back; starting in my pre-teen years explaining how I now see the bad choices I made, even all throughout our marriage. Because I now realize I was ungodly, unthankful, and foolish. I had to go back and see when did it all begin.

 My first mistake was that I was unthankful to those who raised me. I did not want to take advice or correction. I stopped going to Church because of a rumor of a deacon having an affair with another man's wife. I started to hang out with the wrong crowd. I started drinking which eventually led to drug use, all while I was teenager. This continued on into adulthood. The point here is my behavior grew worse and so did my outlook on life. There was very little respect for anyone outside my circle and very little respect for women and almost none for men I did not know. Because I was ungodly and unthankful my foolishness led to all types of behavior. For example, I would go out to get high with the guys and wind up with somebodies' daughter. I was an easy-going guy until you made me angry then, that bad temper would flame up.

 When I was in high school, I would sneak out late at night and go to what I called the bank, back then it was Hunter Street now its M.L.K. Jr. Dr. It was called the bank because it was easy to rob people. To prove how ungodly I was, I thought the bank was a great source to get money to high. I remember watching a cowboy movie where the Preacher had a gun in the bible; so, I took an old novel, "To Kill a Mockingbird," cut the pages out the center of the book and carried a 22 Pistol to school. The vice principal, Mr. Salters would have had a fit had he known I had a gun on the school campus. I had no regard for others and no concern for their physical wellbeing. I was living in my own world and did not really care for anything or anybody outside of my world.

Talking about hanging with the wrong crowd, there was a neighbor named Charlie Porter who was a Veit Nam veteran. He and I along with some others, would drink and smoke weed together. There was this huge house that had four apartments in it. This is where Charlie lived. There were also some students from Morehouse College that lived in one of the apartments. Charlie had the bright idea we should break in their apartment and steal their stuff. We stole their weed, stereo, albums, money, and some clothes.

Charlie was a crook, and I was no better. Charlie knew my folks would not let me bring stolen stuff into our house, so we agreed he would keep it and sell it and we would split the money.

Well, wouldn't you know, he lied to me about the money. Finally, I got fed up and confronted him. As I ran up on him, he pulls a 22 pistol and shot in between my feet threatening to kill me. As I look back, I thank God for Alfred and Heywood, they literally picked me up off my feet and carried me away. Had it not been for them, I would have gotten shot that day. Back then, I considered myself as being fearless but the truth is, I was foolish. I determined that day that I would get Charlie back, even if it took the rest of my life,

A few weeks later I saw him in what we called, "Fair Street Bottom." I took a twelve-gage shotgun and shot him in the face. He was not the only one that got shot, there were some guys shooting dice they got hit too. If I had been closer, I was about thirty feet from him; and if the shotgun shells had bigger shots in them, then Charlie may have died that day, instead, he just got peppered all over the face and chest. I get arrested and charged with aggravated assault the first week of my senior year of high school. I got out of jail the day before our first football game. I went to school and it seemed like everybody knew I had been locked up, even the coaches had questions but they let me play. Meanwhile, I was trying to show this toughness; all the while I was worried if I was going to have to kill this man or would he get to me first.

My mind was not on school. My drinking was getting worst, and my grades got worst also. We went to court twice and my lawyer put the case off by getting a continuance, each time asking for more money. My friends Alfred, Heywood, and I rehearsed what I thought was the perfect alibi. Thank God I never had to use it because I am not sure if they would have held up under the pressure. After all that time had passed between trials, I decided to quit school.

The Bible declares in **Galatians 6:7-9**

7 Don't be misled—you cannot mock the justice of God. You will always harvest what you plant.

8 Those who live only to satisfy their own sinful nature will harvest decay and death from that sinful nature. But those who live to please the Spirit will harvest everlasting life from the Spirit.

Holy Bible, New Living Translation ®, copyright © 1996, 2004 by Tyndale Charitable Trust. Used by permission of Tyndale House Publishers. All rights reserved.

When you think about an oxymoron, I was praying and asking the Lord to get me out of this trouble I was in and at the same time, crafting a lie that would get me out of the same trouble.

I said, "Lord, if you get me out of this mess I will straighten up, go to Church, and turn my life around; all at the same time still drinking, still smoke weed, and doing THC.

Eccl 5:4-7 NKJV say's;

4 When you make a vow to God, do not delay to pay it;

For He has no pleasure in fools. Pay what you have vowed.

5 Better not to vow than to vow and not pay.

6 Do not let your mouth cause your flesh to sin, nor say before the messenger of God that it was an error. Why should God be angry at your excuse and destroy the work of your hands?

7 For in the multitude of dreams and many words there is also vanity. But fear God.

As the Lord would have it, we got to the third trial and Charlie did not show up. The case was dead locked and I was set free.

Do I remember the vow I made? Yes. Did I keep my vow? No.

After the trial was over, the three of us, Alfred, Heywood, and me went out, drank gin and smoked weed. I pushed the Lord out of my thoughts because I was out of trouble, I did not think I needed Him anymore. How wrong I was.

These events started in 1973 and ended in March of 1974.

Fast-forward to August 1987. I get into an argument with a guy. He comes back to the house I was visiting; I open the door, take out my 25 automatic and empty six shots into his chest. The only reason he did not get all seven bullets was because I shot once out of the window first.

I kept all this a secret from my wife for as long as I could until I knew I would be arrested. I remember the expression on her face when she asked, "What are you going to do." I said, "dead men do not talk." The guy only knew my nickname, but he knew I worked for the City of Atlanta and identified me by a photo lineup. This was in September of 1987, almost twenty-four years to the day for the same charge, within three miles of the same location. It appears God has a sense of humor because He gave me my Jonah moment and brought me back to the place of the vow I made.

Galatian 6:7

7 Do not be deceived, God is not mocked; for whatever a man sows, that he will also reap.

March 17, 1988, I awake from my hangover realizing I must make my promise good. One thing I realize about the Lord, He will never leave you nor forsake you. He will be your shield and great reward.

My life changed.

My heart changed.

I served 34-months on a 15-year sentence.

I went in thinking I was going to have to fight my way through this experience, but God gave me favor with inmates, officers, and even the counselor I worked for. I was released from Rogers Correctional Facility on January 21, 1991. In February 1991, I became a volunteer Chaplin for Fulton County Jail. This is the same jail where in 1988, I served four months.

In March of that same year, I had a key to the Chaplin's

office and codes to the elevators. I served as volunteer Chaplin for 19 years. The Lord has blessed me beyond my wildest dreams, and the beauty of it all is I do not deserve any of it.

 I would like to leave you with this one piece of advice; If you are struggling in life, whether it's relationships, drugs or alcohol or anything else, and you have tried to fix it yourself and it has not worked, try Jesus.

1 John 5:4-5,9-10 NLT say's;

4 For every child of God defeats this evil world, and we achieve this victory through our faith.

5 And who can win this battle against the world? Only those who believe that Jesus is the Son of God.

9 Since we believe human testimony, surely we can believe the greater testimony that comes from God. And God has testified about his Son.

10 All who believe in the Son of God know in their hearts that this testimony is true. Those who don't believe this are actually calling God a liar because they don't believe what God has testified about his Son.

1 John 5:20-21 NLT

20 And we know that the Son of God has come, and he has given us understanding so that we can know the true God. And now we live in fellowship with the true God because we live in fellowship with his Son, Jesus Christ. He is the only true God, and he is eternal life.

21 Dear children, keep away from anything that might take God's place in your hearts.

About Henry

Pastor Henry Eberhart is a native of Atlanta, Georgia. He attended Booker T. Washington High School. He received Christ as his Lord and Savior in 1988. His passion for Christ, the Word of God, and lost souls lead him to serve as volunteer Chaplin at the Fulton County Jail from 1991 to 2010.

He was also part of the Highways and Hedges prison ministry under Bro. Tom Norton. As a member of Enon Baptist Church, under Pastor Gregory L. Pollard, Pasto Eberhart received his licensed to preach the Gospel in 1994.

He has served as the Pastor of Set Free Atlanta since 2003. Set Free Ministry was founded by Sr. Pastor Reginald Robbins. Pastor Eberhart was also commissioned by the North American Board, SBC as a Mission Service Corps Missionary 2007.

Pastor Eberhart has been married to Molley Eberhart for 43 years. They have two children, eight grandchildren, and four great grandchildren.

Journey

LWEENDO HANDIA

I hardly slept that night; I tossed, turned, and tried to sleep. I was excited, scared, and anxious all at the same time. The following day was Sunday, January 17th, 1999; it would be one of the most pivotal days of my life. My bags were packed, and I went over my mental list of everything I needed. My mother took care of all the important stuff. We lived in a large mining city north of Zambia called Kitwe.

I had been accepted to study abroad in the United States of America, which was one of my biggest dreams at that point in my life. I got up early that morning, brought my luggage downstairs, and put it in my father's vehicle; I would have preferred we take my mother's vehicle; it was more prestigious. I understood we had to take Dad's vehicle because it was more robust when driving over the pothole-ridden road to the airport in the capital city, where I would finally board my flight from Lusaka, Zambia, to Atlanta, Georgia. We did have a slight detour as my younger siblings attended a rural boarding school, and I had to say goodbye to them that morning.

As we left home, in our usual fashion, we held hands and prayed; Dad said the prayer. My father was a champion driver; he never drove slowly; we arrived at the boarding school in record time. My sisters, just waking up for breakfast on a Sunday, were equally shocked to hear that their brother was headed to Atlanta to further his studies; they both cried. It was the first time one of us would be separated from the rest of the family by such a great distance.

My youngest sister, who was 10 years old at the time, exclaimed, "One day, I am going to America with my brother too." Mom had packed some snacks to soften the blow, and it worked; we bid them farewell and headed for the capital. In the car, we listened to music, and my parents tried to give me any last-minute advice and information that would be helpful to me in navigating Atlanta. We arrived at Lusaka International Airport around 1pm, just in time for my flight. I hugged my mother to say goodbye, and she had the same teary-eyed look when she dropped me off at boarding school a few years earlier for my secondary school education, like high school in America. Dad prayed again, and then he walked me towards the terminal without Mom; I knew a more brutal discussion was about to be had.

My father said three things to me: "No matter how hard life becomes for you in America, coming back home is not an option." This was particularly important advice. I had heard stories of numerous foreign students who found American life difficult and either gave up and returned or got deported for breaking immigration laws. I was determined to not bring that type of embarrassment to my family. Dad also talked to me about handling my legal affairs sensibly, learning American culture, and adapting quickly. He would know because in the early 70s, he, too, had journeyed as a young man to Germany to advance his studies. As he shook my hand goodbye, he said to me very sternly to call home as soon as I arrived in Atlanta.

I walked away and went on to board the plane, very optimistic. I had two stops before Atlanta, Johannesburg, South Africa, and Amsterdam in Holland. I would arrive in Atlanta the next day, Monday, January 18th, around 2pm EST (10pm in Lusaka, Zambia). I would be traveling for 32 hours, including my 2 stops. I had never taken a journey so long before in my entire life. We arrived in Johannesburg and ran into an aunt of mine and her husband from my mother's side at the airport, which comforted me a bit.

I left Johannesburg and headed for Amsterdam on the biggest aircraft I had ever been on. It was a Boeing 747

Jumbo Jet with two stories towards the front of the plane. I watched new release movies on the flight, and when we got to Amsterdam Monday morning, it was still dark. Inside Schiphol airport, I had a voucher for 100 British pounds sterling to spend duty-free. I purchased a Discman and two compact discs, Celine Dion and Brandy. I departed Amsterdam on a flight to Atlanta on a smaller but much faster plane. Crossing the Atlantic was scary and boring; flying against the earth's rotation meant time moved very slowly, and I was getting to experience some jet lag already. Before we landed in Atlanta, we filled out declaration forms for customs. I remembered this process well from observing my parents on other trips. I knew that I was traveling with a lot of money in travelers' checks; this was not to be disclosed to anyone; this money was for my college tuition and upkeep. I had nothing to declare.

I remember thinking Atlanta Hartfield Airport was one of the most advanced airports I had ever walked through; it was certainly the first with a train service for me. I was able to get my luggage with no problem. I had arrived with ease and was ready to get to the school. I stepped outside the airport, and the one thing I did not think about was my first hurdle; it was freezing cold compared to where I had come from, and I was not dressed for this weather at all. As I found transportation to get me to the school, the driver, who was also of African descent, told me I needed to get warmer clothing and eat more food as I was so Lanky.

That afternoon, I arrived on campus to discover it was MLK day and the school was closed. We had purposely bought the airline ticket to arrive on a business day but did not know anything about US holidays. Campus security was able to get the school authorities to place me in a dormitory with other African boys till the next day, when I could successfully register for school and housing.

The dorm was a 4 bedroomed apartment with a twin bed, a study desk, a chair in every bedroom, a simple living room, and a kitchen. The three boys in the dorm were much older and all from Kenya in East Africa. The oldest of them was clearly the leader, he immediately took charge. He arranged transport with another student who owned a car to drive me to get some essentials and food. I also got a calling card to call my parents and let them know I arrived safely. When I called home, my father answered. I could tell the relief in his voice as he told my mother I was on the line, she put me on speakerphone, and we prayed. I was safely settled in Atlanta.

My name is Lweendo; both my parents come from the Tonga tribe in the southern province of Zambia. In Tonga, my name means "Journey." I had just completed the destined journey of my life, and that night, as I went to sleep, I remember thinking I was all alone for the first time. There is no mommy or daddy to save me anymore. Everything my parents had taught me, I needed to rely on now; I should not compromise who I am for anything. The manhood I was being prepared for arrived instantly in just two days. I had my Bible with me, a King James version of the Bible, my mother bought me for my 13th birthday; I had had it for 7 years. I read it and went to sleep, still excited and anxious about what the next few years would hold for me.

I grew up in a Seventh-day Adventist home; my parents attended church regularly on Saturday, and we also attended prayers and bible study on Wednesday and Friday evenings. My mother taught me my first memory verse, "Children obey your parents" Ephesians 6:1. All my life, I used this tactic when dealing with everyone old enough to be my parent. Both my parents were big disciplinarians, educators, and hard workers. A lot of my upbringing was rooted in SDA doctrine and principles of the Bible. Discipline could be in the form of being grounded or not getting dessert after a meal and as much as physical punishment. I was not fond of physical punishment, so I tended not to veer too far from the path of good behavior growing up. It is especially important to raise your children with some form of moral code, and a guide to use for relating with your growing children can be found in church and the Bible.

I started my manhood-style training as I was becoming a teenager. Suddenly, my parents began making me responsible for simple tasks that got bigger as I got older. I cleaned my room and washed dishes even though we had a housekeeper who did it for me before I turned 13 and still did it for my younger siblings. My father would have me wash cars on weekends or weekdays, especially when I was on break from boarding school. These chores and responsibilities grew to fixing cars when my parents ran a transport business and managed a take-away shop (like a small fast-food joint) that my mother ran in the city. My parents always made sure they had enough work to keep me occupied. This helped me a lot in life; I relied on some of these skills to cut costs and survive as a foreign student.

I have learned two great lessons from both my parents, which led to my becoming a man. I was taught to remember that your best efforts do not always yield the desired results. However, you do not quit; you must take any of that frustration and turn it into fulfillment. Many of our bible heroes had to fail first to find success that was pleasing in the eyes of God. The other lesson was that the son you are today is the father you will be tomorrow. Manhood is generational, not only between fathers and sons but also between family members and men of the village.

My father always said to me, "I must be able to trust you more than I trust myself. As a child, I never fully understood what that meant. I usually got this speech when I was given tasks I forgot to do, half did, or just had some attitude towards his teaching method and training me. My parents and siblings eventually moved to the United States. They relied on me heavily to teach them how to navigate this country based on the things I learned by trial and error or from other well-meaning people I encountered. I finally understood what he meant; he knew that, at one point, my father knew he would have to depend on me and wanted to make sure I had the right qualities to lead our extended family if the need arose. A man must be honest, trustworthy, and responsible in all areas of their lives.

About Lweendo

Lweendo Handia is from Zambia in Central Africa.

He finds joy in devling into politics, global events and world history.

Lweendo lives in Marietta, Georgia

Victim To Victory- Calming the Beast

JULIUS JACKSON

One of my favorite sayings is that you don't start constructing a building on the thirtieth floor; you start from the foundation. Much like that analysis, we as humans aren't who we are today without a foundation. Here's mine; walk a mile in my shoes, if you will.

It all began like any other person; you're born to parents, hopefully, in a perfect world, are married, in love, and you were planned, or, at least, somewhat expected, lol. They are so proud and thrilled that you're finally here, especially for the Mothers, after carrying us for nine months. They can't stop holding and kissing you, staring into your eyes, and whatnot. And as with anything in life, those emotions begin to dwindle because, let's face it, "life be lifeing."

Time and years begin to go by, and you're getting older but can still feel your parents' love, warmth, and affection. My prequel to the story I'm about to share, and when my life changed, is around five years old. My parents, like any others, were still, at this time, very much in love and living a life that was indicative of such. They would routinely have date nights and, quite naturally, needed to hire babysitters. From my earlier memories, my first couple of babysitters were two female cousins; the results of those encounters were magical and full of love.

My life would irrevocably be changed forever when they hired this girl to babysit me one night. The evening started like any other, watching television, playing with toys, and eating snacks. Then, a shift occurred; at the time, I had no possible way of knowing anything regarding or pertaining to a sexual nature. As an adult now, as I look back at that life-altering night, she took out my private part and then mounted me with the intent of some sort of penetration; needless to say, being absolutely clueless and dumbfounded as to what she was doing, I had no erection, nor could I produce one, I was five years old. Unbeknownst to me at the time, this would begin a downward spiral in my life that would last for decades; I had just been child molested, even without penetration; it's inappropriate behavior with a minor!

To this very day, I never told my parents, how do you come up with the verbiage at five years old to explain, or even understand, what you just went through or felt, you can't. Even though I had no idea of what she was trying to do, I remember feeling violated, confused, ashamed, and even scared because she was so disappointed that I couldn't satisfy her; she began to scream and curse at me; I just remember crying, and hugging my Snoopy stuffed animal. I know what you're thinking; it's usually a male that molests another male. However, my journey had merely just begun.

As the years went by, and holding that in, I began to withdraw, always have a temper, and love to get into mischief. This led to my not trusting people, reading a lot, and wandering off into never, neverland, trying to escape the internal shame; things really started getting bad. I would have three more tormentors (MONSTERS) in my life that ultimately shaped me into the warrior I am today. Two male cousins and a lifetime male friend of our family, each, would repeatedly try to have sex with me; on every occasion, I would literally squeeze my butt cheeks with every strength of fiber within me, then threaten to scream and tell an adult. See, at the time, I was either nine or ten years old; they were eighteen or older, so basically, pre-adults. It was always at night when the adults were sleeping.

I was never actually penetrated, but the damage was just as catastrophic! I would never be the same again! It is the lowest feeling for a human being. You know what they did was wrong, but somehow, you begin to question yourself. Am I gay? Did I do something wrong? Did I, in some way, entice them? Your mind goes on and on, trying to find solutions to a situation you didn't create, nor are you to be blamed for. It took years before I realized that I was a victim of some sick individuals who may have even gone through similar childhoods, you know the age-old expression: hurt people, hurt people.

Before these incidents I'm sharing, I absolutely loved life, sports, people, family, etc.. Still, my trust in people was never the same after these events. Their behavior created a monster, someone who was silly, loved to have fun, always smiling, now was sullen, had a blank facial expression, and was way more aggressive-minded. As men, we have bravado, reputations, and male pride; once these things have been done to you, you're left feeling like you were robbed, and now you must prove your masculinity to the world all over again. Someone who only used to fight if provoked or to defend myself was now starting fights. I was acting out in class, disrespecting my teachers and even strangers who were adults. When your life has done a complete 360 from the person you used to be, now questions arise, and people want to get to the bottom of your drastic change.

Here's the worst part about this whole ordeal, not only is there a physical attack that takes place, but where it leaves you mentally is the lowest possible place on earth! Earlier, I stated that you somehow blame yourself, and because your tormentors are family, and you don't want them to get into trouble, you never tell a soul, and that creates other facets of your being and demeanor. After all my bad behavior began to garner unwanted attention, our inward survival as humans started to kick in, meaning how I suppress these feelings and behaviors, yet somehow still save face and not tell on my attackers. You get into denial mode and change the narrative on things; I heard it said once that tragedy is the opposite of comedy, and comedy is the opposite of tragedy.

This would be my new course of direction; instead of seeking help, telling what happened, and miring in deep depression openly all day long, I became the class clown. Why? Because this deflects you and others from your real issues. Surely, no one who can make the entire class laugh, including the teacher, can't be going through anything. And for most of my life, that was my charade, my mask, if you will, to keep those demons and that part of my life buried forever. But that's the thing, unless there's total deliverance, the issue will just manifest in other areas, i.e., becoming a heavy drinker, loving to fight, becoming a whore monger, the more women, the better, inwardly, you're constantly trying to prove that you're a man and a conqueror.

Then you realize your life is out of control, and you're headed to a dead-end, unfulfilling existence. You get older, start to get married, and have children. This was when I decided it was time to get my life back. My right now would determine my future, not my past, not me running from it, but embracing it for what it was; I was mistreated but wasn't defeated. I gave my life to GOD and accepted Jesus Christ as my personal Lord and Savior. This was the best decision that I could have made in my life!!

What I learned, and what I'm sharing right now, is that we battle two natures daily, our natural flesh and principalities of a high, spiritual nature. All good things come from above, from our loving Heavenly Father, and all evil, sin, and iniquity come from the ruler of this earthly world, the enemy, the accuser of the brethren. After you get saved and receive the Holy Ghost, you get this peace and calm that will literally orchestrate your entire being, thought process, decisions, and outlook. You're totally submitted and relying on him to get you through each day. This truly saved my life and, ultimately, will save my family's life, blood-related and not. GOD didn't save me just for Julius because several people are assigned to me, people who look up to me and depend on me. The blind can never lead the blind, and the unhealed can't heal anybody.

My lesson learned is that you're victorious and not a victim; you control your destiny, your past propelled you into purpose, and you are living proof that nothing can stop God's design for your life! We have to meet people where they are and don't be so quick to judge. We all have stories, skeletons in our closet, bones to bury, and crosses to bear. Be the standard bearer in your family, declare that all generational curses stop with you, and affirm that LOVE can and will conquer any hardship in this life. The answer to that peace that surpasses all understanding, comes from our one and only Master, the Messiah Jesus Christ!

About Julius

Minister Julius Jackson is a member at Renewed Minds Spiritual and Development Center.

He is a mentor for Men, young and old, about life from a believer's standpoint, always pointing them to Christ.

He is married to Missionary Mona, together, they have three grown children, Jasmine, Hassan, and Jeremiah.

He and his wife Mona enjoy eating out, bowling, and especially, traveling abroad.

Overcoming Self-Doubt

KELVIN KING

To my children Myla and Kayden,

I dedicate this message to you not just on my behalf but on behalf of my dad, David King, your grandfather, and his dad, Alvin King, your late great-grandfather.

This story represents four generations of the King family, including you! I want you to know who you are and the bloodline that guides you.

This story is dedicated to you. I love you, and I am so proud of you. As of the writing of this story, you both are 11 (Myla) and 9 (Kayden) years old. I hope this story can help you, especially when you need encouragement while facing your fears. You could share this with anyone you believe can benefit from my story.

The moral of this story is to help you understand how I overcame my fears and self-doubt. I encourage you to read this story whenever you are about to challenge yourself to do something new and bold, yet you may fear that you aren't good enough. Here goes...

Your great-grandfather, Alvin, is as far up the family lineage as I have known. Your great-grandfather, Alvin King, was a family man. He was married with four kids. He raised his kids in a nation called Guyana. He was a career man who was a driver on behalf of the Fire Department. I remember him as a loving man with a great sense of humor. As much as he loved to tell a story that ended with a laugh, he was also a huge wrestling and baseball fan! He loved his New York Yankees, and when they lost, he took it as personally as Kayden takes the New York Knicks losing!

Your great-grandfather, Alvin, and your grandfather, David, were the last generations to live in Guyana. They became the first generations of King-men to migrate to the United States of America. I bet their decision to move to a new country required boldness and courage. I am sure they encountered feelings of fear as they prepared to try something they had never done before.

When Grandpa David moved to the USA, he settled and created his family in New York City. Just like his dad, he also had a great career in transportation. Grandpa David King worked as a New York City bus mechanic for over forty years! His fathering and hard work allowed me to be successful. Someday, Grandpa King can share his story and identify times he was fearful yet made bold decisions to overcome his fear!

Thanks to the boldness of great-grandfather Alvin King and grandpa David King, many generations of the King family are enjoying success in the USA. I am an airline pilot and businessman because of their ability to overcome their fears!

Here is a secret about me that I want you to understand. You have seen your daddy do some really bold things. You have seen me fly airplanes and run successful companies. You have seen me speaking in front of thousands of people, and you may think I have no fears. But I do.

I have been battling self-doubt my entire life. I have been fighting the fear of failure my whole life. Fear of failure and self-doubt have been the biggest internal challenges that I have had to overcome.

I have wanted to be an airline pilot since I was 5 years old. For every dream I have had and every passion I have wanted, I have had to overcome the battle within myself. I have always struggled with self-doubt: " You aren't good enough." "You aren't smart enough." "Do not bother trying; you will fail."

These are the thoughts I always had to battle whenever I really wanted to accomplish something important to me. I still wrestle with this secret to this day.

This is why I have a relationship with God. The Holy Bible has three scriptures that saved my life.

Scripture #1:

"I praise you because I am fearfully and wonderfully made; your works are wonderful, I know that full well." -Psalm 139:14.

Scripture #2:

"I can do all things through Christ which strengths me." - Philippians 4:13

Scripture #3:

" Trust in the LORD with all your heart and lean not on your own understanding; in all your ways submit to him, and he will make your paths straight." - Proverbs 3:5-6

These scriptures gave me the confidence to overcome fear and self-doubt. Because of this, I have been able to accomplish my dreams, much like my dad and grandfather.

As you begin to make bold and courageous decisions, I want you to continue advancing the King bloodline. You can do whatever you want to do and be whatever you want to be.

You will be challenged by fear, but fear has no power over you. Fear simply reminds us how serious the challenge is and how to prepare to meet it. With God and with preparation, you will always defeat fear!

Our family is rich in tradition. We are known to be a family of hard-working people. We work hard to take care of our families. Someday, you may have your own family to take care of. I have no doubt that you will make the Kings of the past proud! We all already are so proud of you!

You both are the best part of our Father's Day.

As it was said in the movie The Lion King, "Remember who you are!"

You are a King! And I am so incredibly proud of you and excited about what you will accomplish in life.

From one King to another, I love you and will always be here for you.

Love, Dad.

About Kelvin

Kelvin King grew up in Jamaica, Queens and has always been a fanatic of the NY Knicks, professional wrestling, and aviation.

He began pursuing aviation as a career at 14 at Aviation High School in Queens, earning his airframe and powerplant aircraft maintenance licenses.

He continued training at Dowling College receiving his BBA in Marketing and a minor in Political Science. He finished training at ATP Flight School with the ratings and certificates needed to become an airline pilot.

He also served as a cadet in the Air Force Junior ROTC NY 932nd Wing where he developed a professional approach towards life's matters and eventually became a cadet wing group commander, with the rank of Cadet Major.

Kelvin is now a Captain at United Airlines, the Founder & CEO of Alpha Aviation, Inc. and Alpha Drones USA, and he also is President of a 501(c)3, The Sandra Blake Memorial Scholarship Foundation. Kelvin is also an ordained Minister of the Gospel of Jesus Christ.

He is married with two young children, currently residing in Roxbury Township, NJ.

An Answered Call

DEAN LILLARD

When you're raised on a dead-end street by the railroad tracks, you've got to be tough and strong!

For as long as I can remember, I have lived somewhat of a sheltered life. As the youngest of three siblings, an older brother and sister, who are eight and seven years old, respectively, I am the baby of the bunch. I'm not quite so sure that my birth was actually planned by my parents. However, they never treated me any differently from my siblings. I believe that I got away with a lot of things that my brother and sister couldn't. I think that by the time I came along, both parents were older and not as strict with me.

My first true memories began in kindergarten at Nicola Tesla Elementary School on the Southside of Chicago. There was a diverse student population and friendly relationships established during my earliest memories of school. We lived in an apartment on 65th in Dorchester St. While attending primary grades, my parents voiced a sincere demand by emphasizing the importance of education. My report card was closely monitored to ensure I was at the top of my class. With my older siblings being so much older, I always had additional support with learning my lessons.

Gangs soon became a menacing part of everyday life in the neighborhood. One primary gang, known as the Blackstone Rangers, was firmly rooted in the community by terrorizing all of the youth. As a child, I wasn't generally affected; however, my older brother and sister had to be aware of their environment as 8th and 7th-grade students at Wadsworth Elementary School. They often had to carefully navigate the streets to and from school. Our family was blessed that neither was recruited into a gang. At this point, my mother and father determined it was the right time to move our family to a safer community and become 1st-time homeowners.

At the age of 8, in the fall of 1963, we moved into our first home on 75th in Emerald Street. Our new home was located further south in Chicago. This was an era when black homeownership was allowed to expand into several areas throughout the city of Chicago and several suburbs. An example of this era was the movie, "A Raisin in the Sun." Many black families moved into the suburbs of Markham, Blue Island, and Robbins, Illinois.

My mother and father decided to purchase a home further south in Chicago. This area was still integrated at the time. Several white neighbors lived on our block, including our next-door neighbors, the Treyees. This was my first opportunity to experience daily interactions with another race other than my teachers at school as a youth. While at Oglesby School, there were several white students in my classroom. Of course, all of my teachers were white and female. It often seemed that many of my teachers showed a preference for the few white students in the classroom, which I thought was unfair. But I never really made a big deal of it. I was just so curious to interact with people I saw on television programs like "Leave it to Beaver" living next door. I was also able to engage them and learn about them.

Looking back in retrospect, I believe this was my first experience regarding racism. Within less than one year, they all did a disappearing act! And, no white child was left on my block or at Oglesby School. This is a term that is known as "white flight." Behavior like this was quite prominent in many of the areas where blacks migrated and bought homes. This "white flight" became a centralized way of life in our city. Whenever blacks moved into an area that was integrated, within months, houses in the area went up for sale by white homeowners. Businesses also began to leave the area and move further west in Chicago. That also devastated the property values of the homes in these areas, which prevented blacks from ever gaining equity in the values of their homes.

Racism is the "boogie man," meaning he exists, but you don't know how or why. This practice systematically hurt blacks by not allowing minority families to ever increase their wealth. I'm sorry to say that this practice is still prevalent today in many cities and neighborhoods! Another name that we use today to explain this phenomenon is gentrification. It's an ongoing attempt to allow neighborhoods to lose their property value.

Then, middle and upper-class people who have money move in and make substantial investments in homes and businesses. This new real estate investment transforms the community by limiting the residents who have the financial ability and means to reside there because of the new property values. This action redistributes the wealth to certain neighborhoods and groups. Gentrification means no justification! It's a war on poverty that punishes a group of people economically because they were not allowed the same opportunities to establish families and communities.

It was also at Oglesby that I was given a double promotion and advanced a grade level. I'm not sure why that transpired, but I remember my parents discussing whether or not they should accept it on my behalf. After receiving it, the following year, I saw the first young black teacher at my school. This truly shocked me because I had never seen a black teacher, let alone a young black male. Dr. Parker was his name, and he drove a red Mercedes. I don't know the year, but it made a lasting impression on me as a youth.

One Saturday morning, I saw Dr. Parker drive up and enter the apartment building across the street. Later, he exited with one of my friend's oldest brothers, John, who was also a college graduate. I believe John worked for Standard Oil. I was so impressed that I remember telling my mother I wanted to become a teacher and drive a Mercedes when I grew up. It's amazing how much influence a positive role model can have on a young child's formative years.

As I matriculated through my K- 8 elementary school years in 1966, it became obvious to me that we were having some serious difficulties at home. Although my parents had the insight and ability to relocate from a poverty-stricken area into a more integrated neighborhood, we still had our painful family trials and tribulations. My father was a frustrated writer who always wanted to publish, but he often seemed to take out his anger on those who were closest to him. And these memories still linger and haunt me today.

As I grew older, fights became a common experience in our neighborhood, even amongst friends. Many of us had learned about Joe Louis, the Brown Bomber, from drinking our milk at school and home. His picture was on every milk carton we bought. There was also an up-and-coming Champion named Cassius Clay, who later changed his name to Muhammad Ali. We all wanted to float like a butterfly and sting like a bee! We admired him because he could signify but back it up in the ring. We were often manipulated by older individuals within our group to just play box. What often started out as slapboxing often turned into real knock-down drag-out fights.

We had to know how to protect ourselves in the neighborhood. Because my father boxed in the Army Air Corps, he made sure that he taught us all some vital techniques and boxing skills. So, he brought home a couple of boxing gloves to train my older brother and me. Even my sister learned some boxing techniques. Several of my friends soon saw the difference in my ability to "throw hands" and wanted to improve their boxing skills as well. Sometimes, they would come over to the backyard and borrow the gloves to resolve different conflicts instead of fighting with bare fists. It was a great way of maintaining our friendships as well as demonstrating our improved boxing skills. I also began to excel athletically in basketball, baseball, and football. As a result, I now understand why my brother and I would later become boxers in the military.

Both my mother and father were heavy drinkers, which often resulted in arguments and physical altercations. It seemed like my mother and father had fought almost every weekend. However, most of the time, both my family and I kept our dysfunction within the walls of our home when possible. I'm sure that some of my friends knew the truth. Since I was about eleven years old, and my older brother had already enlisted in the Marine Corps, I felt unable to stop the violence when the drinking, arguing, and fights occurred. I experienced a sense of helplessness. I now know that the term to identify my parents today would be "functional alcoholics."

My parents would go to work daily and never miss a day. They appeared to be able to control the amounts of alcohol that they consumed until the weekend when company came to visit. My friends and many neighbors affectionately called my father (Big Brother), and he seemed to relish his newly acquired nickname. His favorite saying was, "Walk tall or not at all." It almost seems ironic that at the end of his life, he was a double amputee and unable to walk at all. I don't believe that my father ever believed in God because he would often say that he was God. And at an early age, I never really understood why he would say those words. I almost cringed every time that I heard him make that statement. Be careful of the things that you say because it appears that, in the end, God got the last word!

Like clockwork, my parents would often begin to yell, and tempers began to flare. That's when my sister and I would hide the knives in the kitchen to prevent my mother from grabbing a knife and fatally stabbing my father. We often attempted to diffuse the fights, but neither of us could stop what would eventually end in a beat down of my mother as well as my father leaving the house. I now understand that many of the fights were provoked by my father as an excuse to leave on a Friday evening and not return home until Sunday evening.

I eventually found out that my father had a girlfriend or two that he spent time with when he was away from home. It seemed as if my mother was relieved when he was away over the weekend. She appeared to enjoy the quality time of going shopping and talking on the phone for hours with Aunt

Eileen or Aunt Sue. Neither were actual relatives but were close high school friends of my mother. And they knew the true essence of my mom's abilities. My father was always a good provider monetarily and brought his check home to ensure that the bills were paid, and there was always food on the table.

However, he would always take a portion of his check to be able to gamble and support his extra-marital lifestyle. My father was not a positive role model for me, and I blamed him for the hurt and pain that he caused my mother. My mother often tried to drink her pain away. I believe that my mother felt the hurt of how society wanted to keep a woman in her place. I would often come home during the evening just to make sure that I put her to bed because she had fallen asleep at the dining room table after she drank too much. Now, I realize as an adult, the pain has to be analyzed and not buried.

When our entire 5th and 6th grades at Oglesby School were transferred to Amos Alonzo Stagg ES, the school had just been built from the ground up. We were the first students to have ever entered the school. As we entered the bathrooms, they still had the white tissue paper covering the urinals and toilets. We had never seen anything like that before. Classes included wood shop with power saws, drills, and high-tech tools we would use daily. We also had a home economics room with complete kitchens.

We cooked our meals on stoves, with the food in the refrigerators, and ate the breakfast and lunches that we cooked during class under our teacher's supervision. However, I clearly observed that all of the students in the school looked just like me. It dawned on me that I may never again see the diversity I had previously seen at Tesla or Oglesby Elementary Schools. However, being at this new school set the standard for what students should experience. In the future, that idea always remained with me. As an educator, I evolved to set the bar of excellence high regardless of the student's socioeconomic status.

I also quickly noticed that I had to steer clear of certain kids in the community to keep from being drafted into gangs. I remember, on several occasions, having to run out the side door after school to keep from encountering gang members. They often stood outside the doors and recruited students as we exited the building after school. Several of my friends were targeted and forced to attend their gang meetings. A couple of my close friends, Tony and Willis, were recruited after school and drafted into the Gonzontoe gang. I'm thankful that they only attended one meeting. I was fortunate and always found a way to escape their recruiting efforts. I often ran out of a back or side door and would sprint up on the elevated railroad tracks in order to walk home or ride the trains.

One Friday afternoon, while walking home from school, I became involved in a play boxing match where the crowd egged us on to box. It eventually resulted in a real fight after things got out of hand. Because of the boxing lessons that I had learned from my father, I beat up Ray pretty badly. I learned an ominous lesson that day. As I continued to walk home, after walking away from Ray's bloody and beaten body, I heard him and the crowd approaching behind me. As I turned to finish beating on him, Ray, who was much stronger grabbed me in a bear hug. He bit a piece of my ear off as I pushed him away. Although I had beaten him badly, I ended up going to the hospital and having to get a skin graph on my left ear to replace the part that he had bitten off. I learned a valuable lesson that day. Never give someone a chance to come back when you're in a fight. Make sure that you finish the fight once and for all when you have a chance.

We also became very adept at signifying and playing the dozens in 8th grade. We often practiced our signifying skills more than in our academic classes at home in order to be prepared to battle verbally when we got to school. We were so good at signifying that we often observed our teachers laughing under their breath at our shenanigans. Many times, no disciplinary action was taken. Remember, teachers used rulers and paddles to discipline us for poor behavior during this time. And most of our teachers were in sororities and really knew how to swing that wood with authority. We found out more about sororities and fraternities as we matriculated to college.

I'll never forget Friday afternoons at Stagg. At around 2:30 p.m., my teacher would close the windows and pull down the shades. Suddenly, you could hear the drums and horns of the bands blasting and patrons screaming in the stands at the football field. Because Stagg Football Field was directly adjacent to the school, the sounds were overwhelming and often deafening. My classmates and I couldn't concentrate on anything else. We couldn't wait to get out of school and sneak into the football game. I remember working with many of my friends digging holes under the fence on Thursday that were large enough for us to slide under the fence. It was an ongoing cat-and-mouse game to be one step ahead of the security on game day, but we always dug several holes to ensure making it into the game. Looking back, many of us who dug the holes to sneak into the games would soon be playing on high school football teams in the same stadium on Fridays. God certainly has a sense of humor.

My mother altered my address so I could attend Calumet High School instead of Parker HS. That allowed me to attend Calumet HS, which was still integrated. In 1968, there were still a few white students attending the school, but by the end of the year, our school was 100% black. That's how quickly white flight occurs. I played football as a freshman and attempted to wrestle. I was pretty good at football, but I wasn't at wrestling. During my high school days, I was pretty much an average student. I often struggled with my academic courses. But, I always seemed to get by with a "C" average. After reflecting on this issue, I believe that the double promotion I received in 3rd grade may have affected me negatively. Because I missed an entire year of school growth, I think it caught up with me in high school. We had several celebrities who went on to become famous.

Chaka Khan and Marsha Warfield appeared in talent shows and were exceptionally talented even at that young age. Chaka Khan later went on to join the acclaimed group "Rufus." Chaka Khan is one of the most prolific R&B singers in the world. Marsha Warfield achieved her fame as a standup comedian and a television actress. The "Brighter Side of Darkness," who sang and practiced in the hallways of Calumet after school, made the hit song "Love Jones." After football practice, I often heard them singing upstairs in the hallway and trying to harmonize with them. Love Jones is still one of the classic love songs today regarding young lovers. Later, Hall of Famer Kirby Puckett, who graduated from Calumet HS, played 13 years for the Minnesota Twins baseball team. He was nominated to the Baseball Hall of

Fame in 2001. His baseball career was cut short because of eye retina damage. He died from a stroke in 2006. Many other celebrities, businesspeople, and politicians graduated from Calumet High School.

As a junior in high school, I fell for the quarterback's girlfriend after we found ourselves in the same social club at school called the LTD, which stood for "Lovers Till Dawn." Linda and I became very close friends, and before we knew it, we had crossed the line and were intimately involved. I thought I was in love. We were always together before, during, and after school. This had a devastating effect on my relationship with my high school quarterback, who had several girlfriends. Since he was the quarterback and I was the tight-end receiver, we found ourselves at odds and were seldom on the same page regarding connecting on passes during the games.

Needless to say, we lost every game during that year in football. And it wasn't long before my girlfriend got pregnant, and I became a father at sixteen. I didn't have an inclination as to what having a child would mean for the rest of my life. My parents tried to help buy many of the necessities for my daughter; however, her family basically took care of both of their needs. It was obvious that neither of us was working a job or mature enough to even accept the responsibilities of parenthood. So, it was only a matter of time before our relationship faltered. We began to argue and blame each other for the situation that we found ourselves experiencing. It was a tough time for us as juvenile parents. We both wanted to make it work, but the odds were stacked against us, and time soon separated us farther and farther apart. By my senior year of high school, we didn't see each other often, and football was my primary objective.

As an athlete on the football team, we always had a very strong relationship because we had grown up together from our early teens. Because of our bond, if one athlete was confronted by any gang member, all of the athletes responded. I guess being an athlete was actually a safety net that kept us from being approached by any of the gangs at school. Not to mention, we had a terrible junior year as a football team, losing every game. We vowed that our football team would win the Blue Green City Championship during our senior year 1972. It was at this point that Tony and I mended our ways and came together as a team. We were known as the "Blue Machine and Wild Bunch."

We had one of the best offenses and defenses in high school football 1972 in Chicago, IL. We were often written up in the Sun-Times and Tribune newspapers. Our offense, the "Blue Machine", often scored a lot of points per game because we were a well-oiled machine. And our defense, the "Wild Bunch," often kept teams scoreless due to their tenacious and ferocious hitting during games. We had a great year and only lost one game the entire regular season. It happened to be our Homecoming Game. And losing really hurt, especially losing the Homecoming Game! Not to mention, we lost on the very last play of the game. However, we were strong and regrouped! We eventually defeated South Shore HS in the playoffs to win the City Championship football game 56-22. I did a great job catching two touchdowns and a point after touchdown in the victory. However, one of my teammates, Clarence (Smokey), ran for four touchdowns and was selected as the MVP of the game. As we now look back over 50 years and watch the movie "Remember the Titans," we see the similarities between these two football teams.

I truly believe it's time for someone to take up the mantle and write our miraculous story about the Calumet Indians 1972 Championship football team, "The Blue Machine and Wild Bunch." Many of my teammates received scholarships to college because of our athletic prowess. One of my counselors, Mr. Sampson, worked long and hard to get me a football scholarship to Morris Brown College in Atlanta, Georgia. In order to qualify for the scholarship, my parents had to sign over my guardianship to one of the counselors at Morris Brown College, stating that I was now a resident of Georgia. After completing all of the paperwork, at 17, I left the Southside of Chicago in May of 1972 and headed south to

Atlanta, Georgia.

My first experience at an HBCU was unbelievable! Coming from Chicago, I gained instant notoriety. And as a member of the football team, I thought it would be smooth sailing ahead. What I didn't realize is that there was a form of racism in the South that had issues with those who were from the North. Although I made the football team, I remember what the head football coach asked me the first time we met. He asked me, "Where are your brass knuckles and your chain?" I thought to myself, what have I gotten myself into? I wasn't quite sure how to answer his question, so I simply said that I didn't have any brass knuckles or a chain. He stated, "You're from Chicago, aren't you." I knew then that his perception of me appeared to be that of a gang member since I was a Chicagoan.

Although I wasn't a starter on the team, I made the traveling football squad, which was a big deal. That meant that wherever the team traveled, I went along with them. That was a great experience, although many teammates made my life miserable. As one of the only players from the North, except for one other player from New Jersey, QT, I was on my own. Of course, my new name became "Chicago" in a negative way by the time the season began. The team was terrible, and we lost our first eight games of the season. That gave me shock waves because it brought back memories of my junior year in high school, where we had lost every game that season. Now, coming from a championship HS football team, I was more than ready to leave on many occasions, but my brother and parents encouraged me to stick it out.

During the season, I had the privilege of playing against one of the greatest football players in history. Our home game was against Jackson State University. They had a running back named Walter Peyton, who later took on the nickname "Sweetness." We had heard so much about him and his ability to run the football that it was coming out of our ears. At the end of the 1st half, the score was 6-3, with JSU leading. I remember going into the locker room and everyone shouting that Walter Peyton was not all that people had hyped him up to be a football player. At the end of the game, the score was 63-3. Each time Walter Peyton touched the ball in the 2nd half, he ran the ball back for a touchdown. It was like a junior high school team playing against a professional player. At that moment, I realized that I would never play professional football if I had to measure up to his ability. It was not only a humbling but also an eye-opening experience. I totally understood why they called him "Sweetness."

When he ran the ball, he ran with power and authority! It was so sweet to watch him glide and move effortlessly around players when he was drafted by the Chicago Bears football team. So, it dawned on me that I had better think about possibilities for my life other than playing in the NFL. The following school year, I recruited eight former Chicago teammates to attend Morris Brown on football scholarships. All of them accepted. When they arrived on campus, my whole life changed for the better. We were as thick as thieves again, and I didn't have any problems with my teammates from that point forward. I wonder why???

While at Morris Brown, I had an opportunity to meet some fantastic people! There were some beautiful black young women at the AU Center. Some women at the various schools, like Clark and Spelman, were well-off and somewhat privileged. We began to find the ladies at Morris Brown, Clark, and Spelman more significant than practicing on a losing football team. The ratio of females to males on MBC's campus was 6 to 1. On the entire AU Center, the ratio was 9:1. I loved my time at Morris Brown College. We often had concerts like Earth Wind and Fire and the Ohio Players visited our school and the other schools in the AU center.

However, soon the losing football team caused a lot of friction with me and some of my partners from Chicago. We should have been more focused on our classes instead of the ladies. I distinctly remember that "The Brighter Side of Darkness" had just released the hit song "Love Jones." Since I knew several of the group members because they also attended Calumet High School, I knew all of the words to the song. I recall writing the words of the song in a letter to Debra, whom I was dating at the time.

Her response to the letter was amazing. She seemed to fall deep and never realized then that I had written the words from the song. If you have never read the lyrics to the song, it would be difficult to understand why she fell so hard. My friends never stopped laughing, and after I thought about it, I felt kind of bad that I had deceived her. It wasn't long before my scholarship was pulled because of quitting the football team. I also incurred a balance of a few thousand dollars to pay to remain at MBC.

I eventually dropped out in December 1973, just when Atlanta elected its first black Mayor, Maynard Jackson. I remember the celebration that occurred on the evening of the election. We rejoiced, although I wasn't a native Georgian. However, even at a young age, I understood the power and significance of electing a black Mayor. My haste to go to the mayoral victory party resulted in injuring my finger, and I had to get stitches the following day! Needless to say, I never made it to Maynard Jackson's mayoral victory party after all.

During that time, Mayor Richard Daley and his son Richard Daley Jr. were in the process of ruling Chicago with an iron fist for the next decade. The father groomed his son to take over as Mayor, and things went right back where they were as far as Chicago politics was concerned. They called it the "machine" because the day-to-day process of politics kept on rolling along in Chicago until the election. As fate would have it, I got another opportunity to see a black mayor. His name was Harold Washington, and he became Chicago's first black Mayor in 1983. He was a breath of fresh air, although it was only for a short season.

After leaving Atlanta and returning to Chicago, I began dating and eventually met Kim over the summer. We started to see each other on a daily basis. It was inevitable once again that since neither of us were practicing safe sex, she became pregnant. I refused to have another child out of wedlock because I wanted to do it right and accept the responsibility of being a father at the age of eighteen. She was sixteen and still in high school. After meeting with her mother and grandmother about our plans, they decided to give her permission to marry because she was underage.

My brother gave me great advice since she was pregnant and I had no job. As a former Marine Sgt. who served two tours in Vietnam, he recommended that I join either the Air Force or the Navy. Since I wanted to travel, I enlisted in the U.S. Navy for 3 years of active duty and 6 years of Reserves. After boot camp at Great Lakes, IL, I was given orders to join the

USS Blandy, DD943, in Norfolk, VA. It was a naval destroyer that held about 300 men. After completing radioman school in San Diego, California, I returned to the ship and made a Mediterranean cruise, on which we visited France, Turkey, Africa, Spain, and Italy.

The experiences were amazing and quite surreal. The different cultures, especially the women, were so beautiful that I had to remind myself often that I was a married man. But on several occasions, I didn't hold true to my commitment as a dedicated husband and faithful partner. What I didn't know then was that my wife exhibited some of the same behavior as a lonely, young, vivacious woman with a young child and alone in Chicago.

Our relationship was extremely volatile. We would often argue, and it would often become physical. This is how I learned that a husband should control his wife. My father had exemplified a terrible model for me to learn as a young man and how to treat a woman. After returning from the Mediterranean cruise, my wife and I attempted to reconcile our marriage and make it work, but the arguments and aggressiveness only continued. I even moved my wife to the various places where I was stationed, from Virginia and Boston to California. However, things just never seemed to work out in our favor. While stationed in Norfolk, VA, I received a message to call home.

Once I called, I found out that my brother had fallen down the stairs at home, suffered an internal injury, and passed in his sleep. I don't remember a lot after my phone conversation with my family, but I went back to the apartment to get my friends who were visiting and take them back to the base. During our trip back to the base, I remember losing control of the car and crashing. As a result, the driver of the other vehicle was killed. His name was Michael Lloyd Jones, and this tragedy still weighs on me today. I wish that there was something that I could do to go back and change the course of my decisions on that night. It's something that I will have to carry with me for the rest of my life. Only God can give you the peace to endure such tragedies.

During my time on the Blandy as a radioman, I experienced many instances of racial slurs, from being called a "Spear chucker" to a nigger! However, I met some amazing friends from all over America. Although we don't keep in touch, many have made an everlasting impression on my life, and I appreciate them. After serving my enlistment in the US Navy, I was honorably discharged.

I soon relocated to Prescott, Arizona, to live with my Aunt Cordelia and her only son, Skip. He was my only cousin on my mother's side. Our birthdays are actually only two months apart, Skip being the elder. My wife and I even attempted to give our marriage another go. After finding out that she was not interested in salvaging the marriage in Arizona, we both agreed to dissolve our marriage, which ended in divorce. It was obvious that although our intentions may have been good initially, at the ages of eighteen and sixteen, we were two kids who were making grown folks decisions.

We are still friends and have a great daughter, DeKima, a certified Special Education Teacher in the Chicago Public Schools educational system. She appears to be following both my sister's and my footsteps in the career of education. I'm so proud of her and the achievements that she's made. I have six wonderful grandchildren. Kwon is working to provide a life for his family. Keenen is in the US Army and married with two children. Karon and Kaylise are presently in college and working to graduate and attend graduate school. Warren is a hard worker who works for the school district in building management. And China is a freshman in high school.

At this point in my life, I traveled to Los Angeles, where I lived a fast life for a couple of years. While living in LA, one of my friend's parents was close to Chaka Khan, and we met again. She didn't remember me, but she attended Calumet High School in 1969, and I reminded her. She was awesome then during the talent shows in which she sang. Now, she is a major star and recording artist. I quickly realized that if I continued to keep up that lifestyle of selling and taking drugs, I would either end up in jail or even worse.

I desperately needed people in my life who loved me and had my best interest at heart. So I soon left California and returned back to sweet home Chicago. At the age of 22, I was really struggling to determine my future plans in life. So, I enrolled in Olive Harvey College and selected to complete a Liberal Arts Associate Degree. While at Olive Harvey, I was on the security force and worked alongside several Chicago Police Officers, including one of my brother's former CPD partners.

As a veteran of the Navy and a student, I was accepted by the team immediately and soon became a supervisor of the security force. I remember seeing an old high school friend walking down the street on my block. There was something so different about her that I asked, "Barbara, why do you look so different." I'll never forget her response. She said, "I'm saved and filled with the Holy Ghost." It was amazing because I had never experienced that type of demeanor before in someone. However, years later, I saw it again and recognized what it actually meant. Upon graduation from Olive Harvey, I transferred to Chicago State University, where I attempted to follow my sister's career path as a Chicago Public School educator.

Dr. Diane Jackson has been a great inspiration for me to follow, and I appreciate and love my big sister. I didn't know it then, but I had a calling on my life to work with children. One of my goals was to be a high school football coach because of my love for football. While attending CSU, I was fortunate enough to remember my teachers at Stagg School, who were sorority sisters. I noticed several fraternity organizations on campus. ONE fraternity really stuck in my mind. I remember going to one of the interest meetings of Kappa Alpha Psi Fraternity.

I was hooked, and after several months of pledging and hard work, I became a member of the greatest fraternity, Kappa Alpha Psi. Our line, The Twelve Assassins, was the largest line that has ever crossed the "burning sands" at Theta Zeta, Chicago State University. Our bond is still strong today! We keep in contact weekly and have a yearly dinner in January to commemorate our anniversary. After 43 years, I still love my Ships! Now, I understand why the sorority sisters who were my teachers at Stagg ES were so close. Their experiences were unique and connected them for life.

Before I did my student teaching at Healy Elementary School in Bridgeport, my college advisor called me in for a private meeting. He informed me that he was going to send me to Bridgeport and wanted to know if I could handle some of the racial tensions that I would surely be facing. He stated that as a veteran of the US Navy, he believed that I would do a fine job, but he wanted to know if I was up for the challenge. He stated that if things worked out, he would send other student-teachers to the area to complete their student-teaching opportunities. After completing my Bachelors in Education, I worked as a school teacher in the Chicago Public School System. I began to coach basketball in one of Chicago's most racially divided areas, "Bridgeport." This was an area where, as blacks, we could move in and out of the community during the day; however, we weren't welcomed in Bridgeport after dark. They had an unspoken sunset law, which was part of the Bridgeport culture.

On one occasion, after the school's basketball game at the park district around the corner, I encountered several youths in the locker room. My safety was in jeopardy because it was turning dark outside, and I should have already been gone. But as the basketball coach, I wanted to ensure I met with the team in the locker room downstairs to give them a pep talk. I'll never forget one of my students, George, who told the teenagers and young adults that I was cool, as well as the coach and his teacher at the school. If not for George, I may not have made it out of the locker room in one piece. I left the gym with an urgency to get home safely that evening.

That was also the end of my basketball coaching in Bridgeport. I later found out that George, who vouched for me at the gym, was important. His father was part of the leadership in the Bridgeport area and well-respected by members of the neighborhood. He was affiliated and connected with the powers that be in Bridgeport if you know what I mean. George even offered to have his father sell me a car due to the age of my vehicle. I was tempted, but I was afraid of what else might come along with the car. I respectfully decided to pass on the offer.

Not long after that incident, I was moved to another school in the Chicago Public Schools system. Because I wasn't a certified teacher then, I was accustomed to being moved from school to school. I had begun to enjoy being "bumped," as the school system called it, to another school. It seemed that at every school, there were young women who were lonely and looking for meaningful relationships. I had my share of relationships, however, none of them were ever serious enough to consider marriage again. After my fifth year of teaching, I was notified by the Board of Education that my salary would be frozen due to being an uncertified teacher. I soon took and passed the NTE (National Teacher's Exam), and I became a certified teacher. My salary would continue to increase yearly, and I would have the stability to remain at one school. I was transferred to Luke O'Toole Elementary School, where I stayed for the next 9 years. I loved my students and attempted to teach them everything that I had learned in my lifetime.

I also taught GED classes for Dawson Technical Institute at night on 39th in State Street during this time. Over 40 years later, I still hear from some of my former students from O'Toole Elementary School via Facebook and Twitter. They appreciated that I challenged them to learn content that would transform their abilities in math for life. I began teaching my 5th-6th grade class the same concepts I taught my GED students. The previous year, many of my students were at least two years below grade level in Reading and Math when tested on the Iowa Test of Basic Skills. After teaching the students that year, some tested at the 10th and 11th-grade levels in math. Several of them had improved multiple grade levels.

Because of their accomplishments on the test, it seems to have caused disbelief that black minority students in Englewood could accomplish so much in a year. One day, I was summoned to the office to meet with members of the State Board of Education. They couldn't understand how so many of these black, socio-economically deprived students made such gains on the math test. Several students also showed improvements in reading, science, and social studies. I was informed that all of my students would be retested again because of the levels of success that they had achieved. The State Board of Education felt that there was a discrepancy in their scores that needed to be explained. As I walked back up to the classroom from the office, I remembered speaking to my class and informing them that the State Board of Education didn't believe their scores could be so high. Therefore, they would have to be retested on the Iowa Test of Basic Skills. I remember telling them that the main test was always the most difficult. I assured them that many would score even higher on the retest. And guess what? Most of the students scored as high on the retest, and several of their scores even increased in other areas.

The following school year, I was moved out of the classroom and placed as the math coordinator for the school. I missed being in the trenches and challenging the students to excel as critical thinkers. Many of the students still remember some of the engaging activities like the "Token Economy." I loved to challenge students to show what they know. Every other Friday was payday for the teachers and staff. So, I allowed the students to earn a little pocket money of their own if they were the last ones standing after the battle of the curriculum.

It became such an important event that the students knew my payday schedule better than I did. It wasn't so much the money that they earned as much as it was the challenge of being the best at memorizing and identifying information by thinking critically. I now realize that several students have become doctors, lawyers, engineers, politicians, business owners, and professionals in every field of human endeavor. I'm so proud to have been part of the educational journeys of my O'Toole students. I still love and miss you!

It was also while I was teaching at Dawson Technical Institute that I met the most amazing woman who changed my life. When I first saw her, I knew she was special and needed to get to know her better. I had only seen this demeanor once, several years earlier, with my friend Barbara, and I knew it when I saw it!

It was the Holy Spirit, and He fascinated me. I was drawn to her from the first time that we met. She also taught evenings at Dawson after working a day job for a construction company. After learning more about her, I realized she had gone to high school with my cousins in Pembroke, IL. One of my cousins reminded me that I had seen her once while visiting him in Kankakee. She was coming out of the Jewel grocery store with two daughters, Jewel and Jacinda. One was about five and the other about two. I remember speaking to her, and she simply ignored my advances and ushered them into the car. I remember thinking then that she was someone who I would like to get to know much better.

When I saw her again at Dawson, she walked with class and a sureness of her purpose. While working in the evenings at

Dawson, I recall asking her if she was married. She asked me if it was written on her head whether or not she was married. I asked her that question because she appeared to be the marrying type. I am under the impression that men really know within three months if a woman is someone that they want to marry. Or are they just someone you would enjoy spending quality time with as a girlfriend to date and have a good time with. And once you make that distinction, it's time to make a move.

So, I did my homework and investigated Annice to find out all about her. I even wanted to attend church with her because she always seemed so happy when I visited her on Sunday afternoons. I felt that there must be a man at the church who was also vying for her attention because of her happiness. So I attended the Apostolic Church of God on 63rd in Dorchester with her one Sunday. I must admit that my intentions were to find out if there was another man with whom I was competing for her attention. After careful observation, I didn't see anyone who posed a threat to our relationship.

During the service, the choir was outstanding! I had never heard singing like that before although I wasn't an avid church member then. Bishop Arthur Brazier preached a great message, but it was his alter call that really had my knees shaking. As I watched many individuals stand and approach the front of the church for prayer, almost all of them went down the hallway and got prepared for baptism. I kept telling myself, I wish he would hurry up and finish. But he just kept on going, and the people in the congregation kept getting up and heading to the front of the church for prayer and baptism.

At the conclusion of the service, I informed Annice that I really enjoyed the choir. She stated that the 11:00 am choir was even better than the 9:00 am service. The singing was so profound that I said I wanted to attend the 11:00 service. I also wanted to see if my competition might attend that service instead of the 9:00 am. I attended the 11:00 am service the following Sunday, and she was right! The choir was even better than the earlier service. This time, I was more focused on Pastor Brazier and his message. He was a real man's man, and I received it.

During his alter call, it was more profound than the previous week's. There were so many people who gave their lives to Christ that I couldn't even count them all. Before I knew it, I was up out of my seat and heading toward the front of the church. However, I went through an additional row of seats before going down for prayer. Everyone was trying to figure out just where I was heading. I didn't know then, but I know now that it was Satan trying to prevent me from going down the aisle for prayer and baptism. That date was Sunday,

November 6, 1988, when I gave my life to Jesus Christ and received the Holy Spirit. Annice never told me that she was praying all the time. She later informed me that she wouldn't have married me had I not given my life to the Lord. We were married approximately 6 weeks later, on December 18, 1988.

Soon, my mother passed, and my father had to be confined to a nursing home. Because my mother was constantly taking care of my father, she had inadvertently stopped taking care of herself and developed cancer. By then, the cancer was at stage IV and had metastasized throughout her lymph nodes. She really took care of my father due to his stroke and becoming a double amputee. My prayer is that she received salvation before her death. On several occasions, we prayed with her to receive Jesus Christ. Through perilous times, my mother was faithful to my father and diligently cared for him until her death. They had been married for over 50 years when she died.

Soon, we had to sell the house and place my father in a nursing home. It was at this time in my life that I was recruited to work as an educational sales consultant for Kinney & Associates. Our company trained schools on aligning their curriculum, creating assessments, and data management systems. My job was to market schools and sell our services. It was a lucrative job and allowed me to travel all over Chicago and the suburbs. Because of my job's flexibility, I was able to set up my schedule so that I could visit my father whenever necessary.

Looking back, I now realize that when you have a relative in the nursing home, it is important to alternate your schedule so that the staff doesn't know when you will visit your loved one. It also makes the staff pay closer attention to the needs of the patient. I established a great rapport with his caretakers to ensure he was well cared for at the facility. Then, one evening, I received a call from the nursing home informing me that my father had passed. Upon calling my sister and informing her, I went to the nursing home to say my last goodbye. So many emotions flashed through my mind regarding my life experiences. Love, hurt, pain, and his salvation were major uncertainties. God gives us all an opportunity to gain His salvation, but we must accept it.

Now, Annice and I have been married for over 35 years, and we're still on our honeymoon. Jewel and Jacinda have always been a blessing to me and have always treated me like a dad. Jewel is a nine-time Emmy-nominated producer and a Social Justice advocate. I know that Jewel is a treasure and will be a great wife and mother. Jewel, please continue to wait upon the LORD because Boaz is searching for you!!

Jacinda is a corporate anthropologist. She also pledged Delta Sigma Theta and married Dave, who pledged Kappa Alpha Psi. I'm so happy she followed my advice regarding marrying a Kappa rather than an Omega. (Smile) They have 3 sons, Malcolm, who is married to Dr. J, who is a pharmacist, and he is also a teacher in Texas. They are soon-to-be parents with their first child. Matthew is also a member of Kappa Alpha Psi Fraternity (3rd Generation), graduated from West Point, and is a 2nd Lieutenant in the Army. Marcus is in college at Georgia State University and enrolled in the US Army's Officer Candidate School.

Over the years, Annice and I have learned one crucial aspect of a Godly marriage. I put her before me, and she puts me before her, and we both place God first in everything! I have truly had the experience of knowing what true Godly love represents. During this journey through life, it is important to know and understand your purpose. Without allowing God to lead and guide you along your path, you will never realize the plans that HE has for you.

Now, as a retired elementary and middle school principal, I have an opportunity to work with and mentor new TAPP teachers entering the teaching profession. I want to instill in them the love an educator must have and possess to truly teach the whole child, not just the curriculum. They must answer the calling of their lives. Although I have experienced some difficult and challenging times, Annice and I are always on one accord. God has allowed us to experience a love that honors Him and exemplifies His love for the church.

Over the last two decades, I have been a member of the Brotherhood Prayer in Chicago, IL, and Fayetteville, GA. I still maintain a brotherly love built on trust and holding one another accountable with Brother Thomas in Chicago. I thank God for the relationships that HE has allowed me to acquire during my lifetime. As I continue this Christian journey, I never want to forget the day I received the Holy Spirit and how He holds me accountable for always telling someone how good God truly is in all situations and aspects. And the journey continues!

(Proverbs 3:5-6) "Trust in the LORD with all your heart; and lean not on your own understanding. In all your ways acknowledge Him, and HE shall direct your paths."

About Dean

Dean Lillard is a retired educator for over 40 years. He is currently an educational consultant for the Griffin Reginal Educational Service Agency, RESA, where he mentors Georgia Teachers to receive their state teaching certification. Over his career in education, he has always strived to challenge students to think critically in order to reach their full potentials by heading in the right direction.

Dean was born in Chicago, Illinois on the south side, and is a product of the Chicago Public School System. He received his Bachelor's, Master's, and Type 75 Administrative Degrees from Chicago State University, which was founded as Chicago Teacher's College.

His goal in education is to impact both students and teachers to achieve greatness by focusing on the "whole child" and not just the curriculum. Dean has served as a Teacher, Math coordinator, Curriculum Consultant, Assistant Principal and Principal in both Illinois and Georgia where he still communicates with many of his former students. Dean is also an Honorably Discharged Veteran from the United States Navy, a member of Kappa Alpha Psi Fraternity, Incorporated, and a mentor on the Men's Prayer Team and his local church where he helps mentor men to take their rightful places as the "head and not the tail" of their homes.

Dean has been happily married for over 35 years to the love of his life, Annice. He loves reading interesting books and articles, working in the yard and garden, and cooking all types of meats on his barbeque pit. Dean is thankful to his LORD and Savior Jesus Christ for allowing him to be part of these great men as they "Journey from Boy's to Men.

Let Up For Nothing, Slow Down For No One

BOB MACKEY

Born into poverty in the small town of Center, Georgia where he soon learned that tough times don't last, but tough people do. Raised by his grandmother, uncle, single mother, single stepdad, and "whoever was off work at the time," Mackey soon realized that the odds were stacked against him. Like many at-risk youths, Bob was in danger of becoming a dropout statistic, and that he did. Despite being placed in an academic program for gifted students at an early age, Bob spent much of his school days in in-school suspension.

By the age of 15, Bob was well on his way down the road to failure, affiliating with the wrong crowd and neglecting his once-promising educational future. But failure was not an option! Bob attended Clarke Central High School and became the first and only child out of his six siblings to drop-out of high school which fueled his passion to become the only sibling to graduate from college, receiving his Bachelor of Science in Criminal Justice. Bob's record of service to youth is impressive for such a young man and has become a hot commodity in the field of youth development and executive services.

Reflecting on my journey to manhood, I've discovered a powerful lesson: the transformative impact of positivity and purpose-driven action.

In a world often with challenges and uncertainties, cultivating a positive mindset has been instrumental in shaping my outlook on life. It's about choosing to see the beauty in every situation, finding silver linings amidst adversity, and approaching each day with a sense of optimism and hope.

Positivity isn't just a passive state of mind; it's an active choice influencing how I engage with the world around me. It's about radiating kindness, spreading joy, and lifting others through words and actions. By embracing positivity, I've learned to foster deeper connections, nurture meaningful relationships, and leave a positive imprint wherever I go.

Alongside positivity, I've realized the importance of living with purpose and intention. It's about aligning my actions with my values, setting meaningful goals, and channeling my energy toward pursuits that bring fulfillment and meaning to my life.

Living with purpose inspires me to pursue my passions wholeheartedly, to challenge myself to grow and evolve, and to make a difference in the lives of others. Whether it's through acts of service, creative expression, or personal development, each day presents an opportunity to contribute positively to the world around me.

As I continue to journey through life, I'm committed to embracing positivity and purpose as guiding principles. By choosing optimism, spreading kindness, and living with intention, I strive to fulfill my potential and inspire others to do the same.

About Bob

An ambitious professional executive whose mission is to improve the lives of others.

Mackey is the idealist and the founding inventor behind the product, Yono Clip. Mackey touts an impressive record of service to youth dating back to 2005-2010 when he worked as a Juvenile Probation Officer for the Department of Juvenile Justice and the State of Georgia.

For the past 15 years, Mackey has held many leadership positions, including the Regional Director of Education, Senior Club Director, and Director of Training for the Boys & Girls Clubs of North Central Georgia/Metro Atlanta, where he has been credited for providing a record amount of academic scholarships to underprivileged youth, increasing graduation rates for students by 87%, decreasing school discipline referrals by 50% and decreasing juvenile delinquency rates by 30%.

In 2017, Mackey was unanimously named the President & CEO for the Boys & Girls Clubs of North Central Georgia (Budget size – $2.7 million managed up to $7 million dollars in federal funding).

Mackey has spoken before over 65,000 youth and adults internationally, implementing successful academic and character building programs he develops for schools and community organizations which has led him to the founding of The Hyped For Education Conference, The Power of the Knot and the Power of the Purse which has been facilitated on the island of St. Croix since 2014, in addition to 21 school districts in the US. Bob Mackey has personally taught The Power of the Knot and gifted over 10,000 young men neckties to foster a greater appreciation for appearance. Mackey has provided over $50,000 in scholarship funds to graduating high school seniors, personally provided over 5,000 community service hours, and has partnered with Facebook, Inc. and the Novelis Corporation to enhance the technology needs for the underserved and underprivileged by designing state of the art technology labs in many Georgia counties.

In his efforts to build tomorrow's future, Mackey has worked with many notable community leaders: Congressman Jody Hice (GA-10), Former City of Atlanta Mayor Kasim Reed; Attorney J. Tom Morgan; Judge Horace Johnson, Alicia Phillips Past President of the Community Foundation of Greater Atlanta; David Johns of the White House Initiative on Educational Excellence for African Americans, Jim Clark; President of Boys & Girls Clubs of America. Mackey has been selected as a Commencement Ceremonial Speaker for many colleges and professional institutions.

Bob has been recognized on many local and national media platforms including being nominated as a Champion of Change for the White House Initiative and as a Top 10 Emerging Leader for the Boys & Girls Clubs of Georgia. Mackey has earned the endorsement of Mr. Evander Holyfield, ESPN Reporter/Author Mark Schlabach, the Steve & Marjorie Harvey Foundation, NBA Professional Football Athlete Rennie Curran, and many others. Mackey is a published author of Outliving Their Expectations, Teens & Tweens Under 18, Far From Being Simpleminded, The Upside Down GOAT, and a magazine series for black families. In 2010, Mackey nominated a family for Extreme Home Makeover and watched the community come together to build a home in seven days on national television!

From Chubby to Vision

CALVIN MANN

As a young boy, Calvin T. Mann (me) was always inquisitive. I experienced a lot during elementary school, and I am here to tell you about the vision God gave me. I remember being gifted and shy at the same time. As a young man, I would venture down the street and play. Food was a huge part of my life. Once my father and mother divorced, things were different. The single household was becoming normal at 20418 Prairie St., Detroit, Michigan, during this time. This was also around the time we would encounter the gang environment.

My dad was gone, and as a boy of eight to ten years old, I was always chasing after my father. This was normal for me.

What's crazy is that it wasn't until I was fifty-six years old that I learned from my uncle, Rudy Hawkins, that I was my father's favorite. One day, a gang approached us while a friend was moving out of his home. They jumped out of the car they were in and started jumping on me to initiate me into the gang. I remember grabbing the first person, who at the time I thought was a friend of mine and putting him underneath me while they jumped on me.

I remember going home that night and my mom saying, "You don't need to be a part of a gang!" "We are a gang!" It was absolutely about us being a united family. You see, our neighborhood was converting to what is typically prevalent today. Our neighborhood went from very few fights to fights upon fights upon fights. There was another time when my mom had to rescue my brother from a riot at Mumford High School. This was around the time in 1977 when we would have to move.

In middle school, I would encounter all kinds of new friends, leaving behind the old eight-mile and moving into the new eight-mile, which in Michigan is called Oakland County, one of the richest counties in the nation. However, the area where we lived wasn't so rich financially but rich with good people. I grew up with a different type of freedom, allowing me to learn much more.

There are so many stories that I can tell of how high school sports, coaches, relationships, and opportunities would shape the rest of my life, especially from a negative point of view. I would turn what was given to me into something more precious. In my senior year at Ferndale High School, it was a big deal when Governor Blanchard came to our school. We also had a number of high-profile athletes. I learned that the high school I graduated from had the same name as my mother's, which was Ferndale, MI, Royal Oak Township Eight-mile. Those areas shaped my life in an unexplainable way.

Then, life would hit me. At eighteen or nineteen years old, I learned that I was truly a good person. According to my parents, that was the makeup of who I was. My mom and dad were good people, my brothers and sisters are all good people, and so were my aunts and uncles. We were taught not to steal and to earn our way. I was also taught to make sure that I was a quality husband, but when it was time for me to go to college, I was broken and hurt. I had been off and on with a young lady during high school. In some ways, I pretended to be hurt because that's what I thought I was supposed to do, but being who I was, a lot was about being heard.

It was the summer of 1984, and the Detroit Tigers were playing in the World Series. I had recently been kicked out of college, so I had to stay in the dorm room with a friend until I figured out what I would do because I did not want to go back home. You see, back home was my brother, who had just gotten married. They had moved in with my mom and siblings while my other brother and I were off to college. Since I had been kicked out, I couldn't go back home, so I came up with a plan. I executed the plan and was able to get through that rough time. Having a resilient plan is important because, in case something goes wrong, you can pivot and get back up. As a man, you must be resilient and be able to bounce back from obstacles and situations. It's not always easy for a man. You have to be able to handle some tough things and make quality decisions.

As a man, you can't be emotional when making those decisions. You have to have a place where you can cry; you have to have a friend you can count on. You really can't stay down because that is a failure. At 20, I figured out a plan to help me get back on my feet after being kicked out of college. At 23, I became the youngest varsity basketball coach. I was overwhelmed and shocked that I had been chosen. Many people at the time saw it as a bad thing and wanted me to fail. Coaching girls' basketball would be one of my greatest gifts on this journey. During this time, I met a woman who would change my life. We were friends, and then we got married and had a son. Something happened in my life when my son Calvin T Mann II was born.

Here's where I share it with you, as a young man, to understand how valuable this is. You have to listen because there will be some things you didn't know, so I will share them because no one shared them with me. We leave young men out there as fathers with the idea that they'll figure it out, which is true to some degree. However, my job is not to leave fatherhood where it is for young men on this journey.

A shift occurs when a child is born in your life. That is the cape, the iron, the fortitude you get, and learning and experiencing fatherhood now, you can't forsake it, but you do have to revel in it and learn what your superpowers are as a father. You can't say, "My father was no good, so I decided to do the same thing." You can't say, "My father and I didn't get along, and so that's something that you ignore," Let me tell you, there is nothing more important or a job you will ever have than fatherhood. Imagine if you had the opportunity to really be a superhero, but you ignored it; you had X-ray vision, you had speed like you could be really fast, you could fly, but you choose as a superhero not to do any of those things. What do you think will happen to those gifts?

So, when I became a father, it was crazy. Nothing was more important to me. I rushed out and got a tattoo. I really fell in love with this process, and here we are today. It wasn't until I was a fully involved father when my son was in high school and we were dealing with high school sports and other opportunities. Life was being shaped for him. He was learning about racism and the complexities of how that works. All the little boys around them were learning the same thing, and yet life was difficult.

You will learn as a young man that it is important never to break your covenant, never forget the values you were taught, and never forget where you come from because ultimately, that is how you are impacted in life. Your foundation is important, so remember, if you have a child out there or are about to have a child, you must remember the impact you bring to your child. I have to share this with you because it's very true! Not many of us really appreciate the value of fathers and what they mean to the family and the children.

As a father, you gain wisdom and age at the same time. Twenty years ago, I asked my then-wife for another son. I prayed about it but was curious if I could have another son. I remember her telling me, "Nothing is stopping you from having another son!" So I know how important this is. I became an involved father because it's crucial to know just how important you are as a father.

When my son, Cameron Thomas Mann, was born, I was in a different space from when my daughter, Dominique Nicole Mann, was born. My daughter was born two years after my mother said my next child would be a daughter before she died from a diabetes-induced heart attack. When she was born, I had a different mindset. My daughter is probably my favorite because she's doing her thing; she's living out loud how she wants to live, which may have been birthed in her when my mom passed away. Unfortunately, my mom didn't get to see the numbers, my growth, the things that I do, but the nickname I gave my daughter was Mama. Today, my daughter kind of believes she's my Mama. It's weird sometimes with her, but every father has a situation with their daughters, so shout out to the girl dads.

Now, back to Cameron.

Once Cameron was born, he would take on the same initials as my brothers, my oldest son, and myself. Although my mother was as serious about her sons as she was about all her daughters, she was VERY serious about her sons; I think this was because she was the oldest sibling alive. My mother was a fantastic woman who did some incredible things.

I want to share some wisdom from this journey with you. Teach your children, particularly your sons, and start teaching them early. I got Cameron to read by the age of four, and that came from the perspective of testing the early reading system, and it worked. It worked so well that my son's uncle once told me it was impossible to get him to read by age four. I got him to read by the age of four during his fourth Christmas; I could have had him reading before he was four. Today, my son does exceptionally well. What makes Cameron's story so intriguing is that people saw me purposefully sit down with my son and teach him to read. One thing you can do strategically is sit down and spend significant time teaching your kids to read. This will allow them to grow into incredible people. Our world needs more incredible people!

Here's another thing you can teach your kids or yourself; Make sure your child has a routine. A consistent routine that allows them to improve. A routine will enable them to discover discipline by repetitive action. A routine cognitively trains you to be on time for wherever it is you have to go.

Routine: A sequence of actions regularly followed; a fixed program, that's the definition. It's important for you to get your children on a fixed program, it'll pay off in the long run. They'll be able to make good decisions, and more than likely, they'll go to school every day. You want an everyday child, a child that wants to be something! A child is full of the words you aspire to daily in your home. Sharing this wisdom is what men are supposed to do.

My last story is about love. You need to understand that many of us men have gone through love. Some men have not experienced true love, which has everything to do with who we are as men, setting the stage for our attractiveness. You have to have confidence, which has had to be built from life experiences, including simply looking in the mirror and believing in yourself. Exercise is a must; it's perfect for feeling better and getting rid of headaches, stress, and anxiety. Exercise increases your hormones, which attracts. The same thing applies to testosterone. It builds testosterone, which heightens a lot of that desire. Nothing has changed; women still want men.

In 2009, I heard this voice over the radio, followed it, and I went into a location to meet Heather Miller. She was a centered person. We would become friends, and she would help me in business because it's who she really is. Alright, we both ended up getting divorced. However, it would be January 2, 2015, before I would see her again. I hadn't seen Heather in almost four years when she called out the blue sky. We got together and had dinner as friends. I was ok with the dinner; however, she had other plans, and I said no; I was going through a lot and didn't want her involved.

I was homeless!

I talk about being resilient, and this is another example. I had lost my family and was dealing with that voice and sleeping in the barbershop on the floor. A friend who is a part of my fatherhood organization opened his apartment and allowed me to live. Then, I started getting phone calls and other resources and ended up with a car. During this time, Heather maintained a friendship and decided to be supportive in any way she could, which was smart because I was going through a lot. Time went by, and we finally went on a date in 2016. again, I was apprehensive because I was just coming out of a very long relationship. However, we would one day pivot. I would start listening to who she was and what she was, and in 2019, we would get married, and we are working on our happily ever after.

I am the president and founder of a vision for boys, men, husbands, and fathers, and I'm living in my purpose. Remember, you need obstacles to learn from, grow from, and find your purpose. Now, go find your purpose!

About Calvin

According to Calvin T. Mann, "I learned quickly about the profound impact of fatherhood on one's identity and self-concept. I learned the importance of words and allow them to become my vehicle to spread encouragement. Whether to an audience, in a book, article or through our apparel; what we say and do makes a difference.

" The vision of encouragement has made a global impact and led to a movement which initiated Encourage Me I'm Young, Inc., (EMIY) and Good Fathers Only (GFO) non-profit organizations dedicated to family through supporting and encouraging boys, men, husbands and fathers.

Calvin lives in Michigan with his wife Heather.

Patience, Resilience, Sustainability

The Falsetto to my Key to Life

EPHRAM MARSHALL

Self-empowerment. No validation is needed; only validate
yourself and seek approval from yourself and God for those
who choose to believe.

Consistently inconsistent

When you're self-empowered, you already have all the tools.
Saying be all you can be sounds so cliché but unbind the
thoughts that you're physically restricted, financially limited,
or educationally inept to accomplish ANYTHING in this
world. Unlearn that. We're all born with the same tools, and
only "drive" keeps a border between us and the next person,
no matter the status, just like prejudices.

No one is born prejudiced. That's a "learned" behavior. It's taught. Place two equal-aged toddlers in a room before societal tarnishes and hatred never exists. Anyone can learn or choose not to learn that hatred is taught. It's the same as with anything in life. So, backgrounds, pasts, etc., shouldn't be allowed to place restrictions on the life that's to come.

My biggest accomplishment was becoming a Father. Even at a young age when I knew absolutely nothing. I thrived off what I learned from my Father, some good, some not so good, coupled with my own perception, trial and error; learning along the way but never giving up. The things I needed to unlearn in my journey helped to mold me into a better Father and person. I would (and do) tell my kids and my younger self, you don't have all the answers. Neither will you., reading this.

There's no one-size-fits-all or instruction manual to life. Errors build character, learn from them. Use them and the mistakes of OTHERS to garner succession. I inadvertently remained consistently inconsistent. And no, everything won't be appreciated, whether from the heart or out of necessity. My Father told me you can build a Fortune 500 company, but you can't take it with you, so leave a legacy. Life's lessons that can be passed down are another form of a tremendously overlooked legacy. So, my biggest accomplishment is becoming the man my Father envisioned. Life, religion, finances, business, academics, and even politics...but To "Father "the way I was "Fathered" and instill those same core values in America's next young black youth in the form of my own kids, that's my greatest accomplishment. "Salute Pop!"

Lessons from My Dad

My dad was a wise and strong man who taught me invaluable lessons about life, family, and survival. He instilled the importance of hard work, perseverance, and resilience. He taught me to never give up, no matter how tough the circumstances may be. His guidance shaped my character and helped me navigate challenges with strength and determination.

Navigating as a Black Male

As a black male, my dad knew the challenges and obstacles that I would face in a society that often discriminated against people of color. He taught me to be proud of who I am and to never let anyone diminish my worth because of the color of my skin. He showed me how to navigate through a world that may not always be fair but to always stand tall and fight for justice and equality.

Being a Father

One of the greatest lessons my dad taught me was the importance of being a father. He showed me the value of being present and involved in my children's lives, providing for them, and being a positive role model. He taught me that being a father is a lifelong commitment that requires love, patience, and sacrifice. His example inspired me to be the best Father I could be and to always put my family first.

Success in Life

Through my dad's teachings and examples—good and bad—I learned that true success in life is not just about material wealth or achievements but about integrity, compassion, and making a positive impact on the world. He taught me that success is about being true to myself, following my passions, and never compromising my values. His lessons guided me on the path to success and helped me become the person I am today.

In essence, I've learned a lot along the way and from every angle. I was taught AS a man BY a man...the manliest of them all...but I've raised sons AND daughters and co-raised a host of nephews AND nieces.. so it is not gender specific. I've made some mistakes, sometimes I've nailed it, and sometimes things may have even come across as harsh.. but from a place of love and a place of "Duty,"... I've told my kids, "If you don't hate me at least ONCE in your life, then I haven't done my job!" Those life lessons, I guarantee, are embedded. You'll always have them to come back to when needed, even long after I'm gone. Legacies aren't only physical, material, and monetary. I pray I've left one hell of a legacy.

Pay it forward, generationally.

About Ephram

Ephram Marshall is the owner of a Home Improvement and Commercial Cleaning Service.

Ephram is also the Owner of a small trucking company.

Ephram is a man of faith who believes in family and hard work.

Ephram lives in Atlanta with his wife and children.

Lessons I Learned on the Journey

JEREMY MYERS

Ever since I can remember, I have always felt safe and protected, and I attribute that to my parents. They raised me to be grateful, love God, and treat people how I want to be treated. Although there were some struggles along the way, I took the good with the bad. I was fortunate enough to be raised by both parents.

This gave me the opportunity to see the different sides of where I come from and learn from them.

My mom was always so loving and caring towards me and still is. I remember wiping the lipstick off my cheek from all the kisses when I was little on the way to school.

I love my mother and appreciate her loving heart and how

she always helped others. She taught me to always help others in need and let God's light shine through me. I can recall, on multiple occasions, her giving someone a ride or picking up something for someone. She would say you never know what a person is going through and that one good deed could make a difference in someone's life.

My mom is a real social light and a people person. I guess that's where I got it from. She can converse with pretty much anyone and find things in common. I admire that about her and hope to exhibit those same traits someday.

My mother started off as a probation officer but eventually gravitated to social work and working with children, and this was more of her style. She loved her job and worked very hard to excel in it. Gradually, she was promoted to a higher position, requiring her to be more available. Things were a little different then. I remember her being on call and having to pick different children up from foster care at all times of the day and night. She made it through and retired finally. She still works part-time with children, which she loves.

My father is quieter and more reserved at first until he gets to know you, which is the opposite of mom, but they say opposites attract. He was in the military and fixed cargo planes for the Navy. He met my mother while stationed in Chicago, where my mother is from. They married and moved to Florida, where I was born a few years later. I don't remember, but I saw the pictures of my dad and me standing in front of a black-on-black 88' Maxima. We later moved to Georgia when I was four.

I was a very adventurous child growing up. I remember journeying into the woods behind our neighborhood to see what we could find. We came across all kinds of things like old abandoned shacks, old quarries, and creeks. I was a real explorer.

My father taught me many things less through words and more through action. He showed me things around the house, such as washing the car, mowing the lawn, and other things to maintain a home. I would go to Florida every summer to stay with my grandparents. My grandfather was a landlord and had a couple of houses he would fix himself, and I was his helper. Spending time with him taught me many more skills, such as painting, cutting carpets, and sheetrock. I didn't like it then, but I am very appreciative now for the lessons I learned on my journey from being a boy to becoming a man.

About Jeremy

Jeremy Myers took his passion for painting and started his own small business. Jeremy is the Owner of J.A.C.C. Custom Painting.

He absolutely loves nature and going on long hikes. Jeremy is an avid reader, likes to write and enjoys playing basketball.

Jeremy is very passionate about family and he loves Sunday dinners with his parents at their home.

Jeremy is an amazing father to his four children, Carter, Amir, Christian and Arya.

A Life's Journey

SGT. JAMES PARKS SR.

My journey began in 1952 in a little town called College Park, Georgia, eight miles south of Atlanta. My first traumatic experience happened when I was three years old, playing near a wood burning stove. A hot poker fell on my foot (OUCH!) and to this day, I still have the scar.

I am of the Parks clan of Southwest Georgia, from a little town called Lincolnton; 136 miles southwest of Atlanta. After World War II, my grandparents moved to Atlanta in search of a better life for their family. My grandmother, whom everyone called Grandma, was one hell of a woman.

Looking back, I hate to think what would have happened to me and my siblings without our grandparents. Grandma was a jack of all trades: carpentry, sewing, gardening (she had a beautiful vegetable garden) and cards. She was a stay-at-home mom and an excellent cook. She knew about everything; she raised chickens and made the best wagon wheel cheese. Grandma was also a hustler- selling white lighting (moonshine) by the pint to help make ends meet. My grandfather was as big as life, but everybody knew that Grandma was in charge!

My grandfather worked at Georgia Pacific LLC, a paper and pulp company. Grandpa always drove a nice car. When we were in elementary school, the rule for my brother Gerald, my cousin Grady Lee, and me was to be home before Grandpa, or get the "switch." The switch was a six-foot hedge, sometimes two to three coiled together at a time. If we got into trouble Grandpa would tell us to go get the switch. Sometimes Grandpa would whip us, and sometimes he made us whip each other. Grandma could be heard saying, "Ok Ike, they got the message." Just knowing that we were going to get the switch pretty much kept us in line. The three of us played together and did as we were told. There was one year separating the three of us. I was the oldest, so I had to keep the other two in line.

My grandparents kept the family together. They had four Daughters: Estella – my mother – who was the eldest, Aunt Idella, Aunt Jean, and Aunt Lora Mae. Our aunts were always there for us. Mother did the best she could. She was a headstrong woman who dropped out of school in the fifth grade. She had my older brother, Thomas (we call him Tom), when she was 15 years old. My mother was an alcoholic and would often disappear on binges for several days at a time. I missed her when she would leave us for extended periods, but because my grandparents loved us, we were able to function when my mother was not around.

Growing up in College Park in the 1950s was cool as long as we Black folks stayed in our own section of town. You could be sure that somewhere around the colored section, the local KKK would have a cross burning. It was a constant reminder for Black folks to "stay in your place." Don't get caught out after dark in the wrong place!

I remember four men in our early lives who were role models we looked up to: my grandpa who was well respected in our community; my uncle Ben who was fearless; my oldest brother Thomas who was an athlete in high school (he was the oldest so he was in charge); and our neighbor Mr. AZ Greer – a World War II Army Vet who lived next door to my grandparents. My brother Gerald and my cousin Grady and I played in the back yard where three of our neighbors' properties were joined, and that was enough space for us. The area was full of Georgia red dirt, and when it rained the red dirt was everywhere.

Everyone respected Mr. AZ. I use to go with him to his job at the American Legion. By watching him, I learned about hard work, and to pay attention to details. Uncle Ben was married to my aunt Idella (Aunt Idella was a great cook but not as good as my grandma), and they lived next door to Mr. AZ. Uncle Ben was like Tarzan – tall and light-skinned with long dark hair. He wasn't afraid of anybody, including the KKK! I guess that was because he was very light-skinned and could pass. My uncle was a hunter and a fisherman, and on occasion he would take us hunting and fishing with him if we could keep quiet. My take on Uncle Ben was he was an adventurer; a loner and a rugged outdoor type. Some of that rubbed off on me. I learned early on that it takes discipline and courage to hunt at night; skills that came in handy later on when I was in the military.

Uncle Ben had a hound dog named Blue. Everyone loved Blue. He was a smart dog, and he would hunt just about anything – rabbits, possums, you name it – all he needed was the scent. One convenient hunting and fishing spot was the huge rock quarry and lake that was on the public golf course, less than half a mile from where we lived. We were not supposed to be on that course at night. The only thing Blacks could do on that golf course was caddie. But against the odds, at night my uncle would sneak on the course to hunt and fish.

I remember hunting there with Blue. When my uncle turned him loose, he would quickly pick up the scent, and the closer he got to his prey, the louder he got. At night we would follow the sounds as Blue would tree (a method of hunting) or chase his prey down. The phase, "barking up the wrong tree," comes from this practice. Sometimes, when I close my eyes, I can still hear old Blue, howling as he was getting close to his prey. Sunday was family day, and in the evening, we ate dinner, played Spades, Bid Whist, and watched boxing on television. Boxing was our favorite thing to watch; at that time, Floyd Patterson was the champ.

In 1953, my mother met and married Private 3rd Class James Doris Woods, United States Army. My stepfather had always been quite mild-mannered and well-liked by all who knew him – a well-informed soldier who loved jazz and was a great father. My brother Gerald and I tried to emulate his every move. After marriage, he was assigned overseas to Germany, and took my mother and my younger sister and brother with him. He returned later that year and took me, my sister Johnnie Mae, and my brother Gerald with him back to Germany. Suddenly the world seemed to open up for me. Starting with this trip to Germany, all I wanted to do was travel and see the world.

This trip was my first big adventure. It was exciting and scary at the same time. We flew from Atlanta to New York, then sailed out of New York harbor aboard the USS Buckner, one of the largest military transport ships at that time that was used for transporting troops, cargo and military dependent families. The ship was like a floating city, with thousands of troops on board along with hospitals, restaurants (the food wasn't bad) and movie theaters. There were several decks on the ship; military dependents mostly occupied the second deck, and troops and supplies filled the lower decks.

We traveled through the English Channel, passing the white cliffs of Dover. What an amazing sight! We also saw large pods of whales. Days later we docked in Bremerhaven, Germany – one of the largest ports in Europe – where we took a six-hour train ride to Mannheim. The train trip was very interesting and the scenery was amazing. Traveling through the countryside, following the Rhine River, and seeing the castles and beautiful forests and landscape made a lifelong impression on me and my brother.

My stepfather was stationed with the 51st Mechanized Infantry, part of the 3rd Armored Division, Sullivan Barracks Mannheim. It was truly a life-changing experience. We lived in a large military dependent housing project for soldiers and their families. At the time, all of Germany was occupied by the Allies from World War II. From my experience, the German cities that the US Army occupied were the best – clean and historic.

My stepfather was promoted to Specialist 5th Class. He loved bringing his soldiers over to our quarters on the weekends because they did not have family in the country. We played baseball and other sports in the dependent youth and sports recreation league.

My brother Gerald and I were fascinated by the military. Watching the parades and seeing all of the awesome military gear was pretty impressive. Watching my stepfather in his duty uniform and dress uniform was the deciding factor – we knew we were going to join the Army.

We didn't have a lot of contact with the civilian population. We attended an armed forces dependent school for US service members' children. There were kids from all walks of life at that school, and we all picked up a little German or Dutch. This was also the first time my siblings and I had white teachers. Some were very kind, and some I didn't have a lot of respect for because of they way they treated us.

The German people were very skilled and cultured, and conservative. My stepfather would take us to see different interesting sites around the town of Mannheim. The shops that sold pastries and candies and ice cream were always a favorite. The city was clean, with mostly cobble stone streets, but there was always construction going on. My stepdad told us that they were rebuilding because of the war.

Sometime in 1962, my stepfather got word that his mother had died, and we returned to Georgia. In 1964 the hormones kicked in and I started to become interested in the girls. Sex was on my mind, rock and roll was in full swing, and Gladys Knight and James Brown were popular on the airwaves.
In the eighth grade, I enrolled in Booker T. Washington High School (Go Bull Dogs!), where Gladys Knight had attended. All the teachers were Black – very professional and hard, but fair. High school was really a wakeup call because now I had to stay focused. That was hard because I started to meet new friends and I couldn't keep my eyes off the girls. During this time, I met and began dating Brenda Hann, who would later become my first wife.

I started playing golf at John A. White golf course, and picking up other hustles. I used to go up to Morehouse College and shine the students' shoes, and do odd jobs at Erwin's Market – a little Jewish-owned store up the street from where we lived in middle of the College District, which consisted of Atlanta University, Morehouse College, Spelman

College, Clark College, and Morris Brown College. The owners, Mr. and Mrs. Erwin, would always give me work after school and on weekends.

Gangs were always trying to recruit me and my brother Gerald. We were targets because we didn't join the local gang. When we resisted, they tried to intimidate us. We had to fight or run like hell whenever we saw gang members. Thankfully, when school was out for the year, my mother moved the family to Southwest Atlanta to the Center Hill area in the suburbs.

When the following school year started, my brother and I enrolled in West Fulton High School and became Owls! What I really liked about West Fulton High School was the ROTC (Reserved Officers Training Corps) program. ROTC is designed to teach basic military skills, leadership fundamentals, and career training. The uniform was a big draw for me and my brother. The ROTC program was staffed by two active-duty soldiers

I experienced many "firsts" that year. I met a girl at school and we liked each other right off the bat. My first sexual encounter was with her, behind the auditorium which was also a shortcut to the gym. While visiting my Aunt Jean and her husband, Henry, I picked up some marijuana that fell out of Uncle Henry's pocket. I kept it for weeks before I had the courage to try it. That same year I started driving. I drove my mother's car, although I didn't have a driver's license. At that time, I had a friend named Charles Linder who was a on the basketball team, and my mom would let me take the car if Charles was with me.

Atlanta is known as the epicenter for the Civil Rights movement. Back then it was the main topic of conversation everywhere. We protested and rioted in our own communities. We fought for voting rights, access to public facilities and institutions, and economic and educational opportunities. Years later, we are still having these same discussions. The more things change, the more they stay the same.

I was drafted into the Army in June of 1969, and went through basic training at Fort Campbell, Kentucky and AIT (Advanced Individual Training) at Fort Polk, Louisiana. My first duty assignment was in one of the oldest active units in the Army, A Company 1st Battalion 9th Infantry Regiment, where "Keep Up the Fire" was our motto. My skilled occupation was 11C10 Indirect Fire Crewman in the mortar platoon. I did two tours in Korea and two tours in Germany. I retired in August of 1989.

I fathered six beautiful, smart and intelligent children by

three different and wonderful mothers. Despite all of my shortcomings, I love my children very much. I am impressed with their achievements, and they have all turned out to be great parents and good people. The contributing factor is the way their mothers raised them. My children's mothers were great mothers; I was the selfish one, driven to see as much of the world as I could. But no matter where I am or what I am doing, my kids are often on my mind. Let's be clear- no amount of forgiveness can cover the hardships I caused, or the missed special occasions, births, graduations, birthdays, holidays, football games, or learning how to drive. My penitence has been to try and be a better man.

A funny thing about aging is that it gives one much time to reminisce about what could have been. My journey from being a boy to becoming a man has brought me closer to my family and friends. Reality has shown me that everyone can become a better human being. Much love goes out to my wife Charlene who came into my life when I was at the gates of Hell. She saved me from myself. And to all my children, know that you have come this far, so be proud of who you are. Keep finding ways to reinvent your efforts when you run into roadblocks. Give as good as you get, get closer to the clan, spend more time with your cubs, and leave things better than you found them.

Stay the course and be the master of your own journey.

Sargent Daddy & G-Papa

About James

James Parks is a retired Army Sergeant, youth advocate, community activist, podcast host and environmental justice advocate. Committed to helping improve his community, his passion is mentoring young people. A well-informed community activist, Sargeant Parks – or Sarg, as he is called – is president of the Yakima County NAACP, and serves on the Henry Beauchamp Community Center Advisory Committee, in Yakima, WA.

Sargeant Parks has worked as a site supervisor for the Gang Prevention Intervention Program with The Yakima County Substance Abuse Coalition, where they worked to reduce the negative effects of gang involvement by creating networks and finding common ground with other entities to focus on building protective factors in the community in order to have clean and safe spaces for all people.

Sargeant Parks volunteers with Opportunities Industrialization Center (OIC) of Washington, a non-profit that helps develop alternative activities for youth in destressed communities. Working with other concerned groups in the city of Yakima, Sargeant Parks has served on various boards and commissions. He has teamed up with area churches and concerned citizens to organize community cleanups in District 1 and District 2. He is engaged with local law enforcement to improve law enforcement and community awareness. He has organized youth leadership conferences and is currently coaching youth basketball and golf.

Sargeant Parks is the proud parent of 8 children, and has been blessed with 15 grandchildren, and 4 great-grandchildren. He and his wife Charlene enjoy taking young people on field trips to broaden their horizons.

Life Is A Trip Through Time Without A Suitcase

The gathering of knowledge, understanding, clarity, and wisdom through my journey from Boyhood to Manhood!

DAVID PATTERSON

Our journey from boys to men is a developmental process that starts off somewhat challenging. Yet as the journey progresses, many aspects of our development takes on a life of their own. This causes an individual to be on the continuing pursuit of life and learning. To briefly sum up a life journey of over many decades in a few words will be challenging, but I've come to believe that these brief lessons learned is worth sharing to help save someone twenty years of unnecessary that is nonproductive for the benefit of living one's best life.

My life's journey that has taken me from boyhood to manhood, has been filled with twist and turns, starting from my informative years as a boy, teen and young adult to where I stand today. As a seasoned individual with a more developed wise mind, the primary objective as men should be to become spiritually, mentally, and emotionally mature for the preparation of the next generation of men to come.

However, this ongoing development of knowledge can appear a bit confusing, frustrating and overwhelming at times. I believe these multiple perspectives comes from limited resources and expectation, created directly and indirectly from family, associates, friends, teaching, experiences, education, religion and other associations that we are exposed to at some point in our lives.

These perspectives generated a great deal of expectancy that can cause many false beliefs and ideals. This creates a great deal of taxation when individuals don't gain access to a deeper understanding, which would bring about clarity towards gaining the wisdom needed to help one properly align himself with an individual's true purpose. And if by chance, some of my expectations were fulfilled, no one really explained that.

As life progresses, this gathering of knowledges which should help me be able to distinguish my wants and desires over my needs, which would cause me to understand that through people, places and things over a life time, would therefore generate more unanswered questions that need to be addressed to accomplish the requirement of what it means to be man. However, with limited knowledge, understanding, and short-sighted clarity, the wisdom that I was seeking would elude me, therefore leaving me to be more emotional in my responses, instead of logically proactive and productive fulfilled results.

I will share just a short synopsis of my life wrapped up in the figures that sums up to 24,090 days which totals 66 years and growing. I present these numbers for a specific reason. If we as individuals think about time, which is "the continued sequence of existence and events that occurs in an apparently irreversible succession from the past, through the present, and into the future," It should stimulate the thought or question, about what am I doing with the time that God gave me to become a man? Am I being productive? Am I developing and moving toward spiritual, emotional and psychological knowledge, that is in each of these stages of intellectual maturity?

I asked the questions, "Am I becoming more intelligent in these areas on a daily basis?" "Am I taking care of the host or body God gave me to be utilized, in order to become his servant that serves and helps develop myself and fellowman?" "Am I developing the spirit that God blew into me to be spiritually mature?" In all these questions and more, what kind of son, brother, friend, man, husband, father, community servant will I become? And the most important question is, "What kind of servant will I develop into, in order that I may hear my Heavenly Father say to me one day "well done my good and faithful servant?

All these thoughts run through my mind, heart and soul. Where am I going, as I move from boyhood to manhood? And will I meet these expectations with a level of reasonable proficiency as God guides me through, with the power of the Holy Spirit on this journey, we call life. An artist name Gino Vannelli wrote in his lyrics of the song "Where Am I Going?" (1975) He asked some questions that I believe many men may ask themselves, maybe presented different but carrying similar meaning." Where am I going? Have I gone too far? Where are my eyes? Oh, have I seen too much? Have I lost my touch? What will I be like when my head is bear and my legs are weak? Will I be strong or barely kept alive when I am thirty-five?"

I often like to entertain the above questions; Where I've been? Where am I going? and Where am I now? Looking back on my past, it has been interesting to see how God has confirmed his word to me multiple times that I am truly an overcomer, based on what I have overcame on this developmental journey known as manhood. There has been a series of events that directly affected my path, in many of the aspects I mentioned earlier. Boyhood was filled with ups and downs, that seemed to conflict with things my mother would say to me such as "Right follow right and wrong follow wrong." However well intended as she may have been, those kindhearted views of loving and treating people how you want to be treated didn't play out that way in many of the life experiences I encountered. Like many, I would assume, I have experienced bullying, verbal abuse, and emotional pain; all before I was six.

Now, wondering what kind of children can be so cruel at such a young age. As a singer name Lou Rawl said, "I learned to fight before six, it was the only way I could get along." Being placed in multiple schools because I was expelled from many of them for fighting, which I didn't provoke, but always having to defend myself. And the sadness was that my mother seemed to not believe that I didn't cause these problems at school. Yet these experiences would prepare me for such a time as this.

This preparation I am speaking of would be understanding that "hurt people hurt people," and that I know now as the scripture would tell us in Ephesian 6:12 "12 For we wrestle not against flesh and blood, but against principalities, against powers, against the rulers of the darkness of this

world, against spiritual wickedness in high places."
Understanding this helped me to better handle the darts
Satan would bring.

You see, Satan was so busy coming after me early on in life.
He knew God had a plan for me to share his Good News of
the love he has for us to the world. His attacks came from
fighting with peers, neighbors attempting to molest me, my
female babysitter molesting me, getting hit by a car, almost
losing my tongue to speak, for which a part of it is gone, to
falling on a nail that went into my brain, to losing my sight
and just too many incidents to list. The crazy thing about it
was that I hadn't even reached ten years old.

The lessons were invaluable, developmental and informative
in my understanding. An important lesson I treasure in my
life is that God has never left me or forsaken me and
continues to protect me for such a time as this to share these
lessons I've learned.

Once I reached middle school, a teacher made a prediction
about me as it related to my intelligence level, (which I
questioned), since I was double promoted twice; because in
the sixties the school system allowed such a thing to happen.
Therefore, being the youngest student in my class I would
discover later that in truth, I was head of my class. However,
she stated among my peers how great they would be, and

how they would move into these roles as a teacher, a scientist, engineer and other acceptable professions but for me, I would be a factory worker with five kids; which everyone saw as a job that was less desirable.

The kids laughed and shamed me for some time but I had a positive attitude back then, which would keep me going strong for years. I stated to everyone that her view of me was fine, because I saw myself differently. Being a kid, I was always planning for my future. My reply was interesting for a child, I stated that I would build a business, whereas I would buy up five houses, rent them out and sell them before I was 25 years old and live great. This didn't come to pass but what did happen is, I graduated high school at 16.5 years old, went to college, joined the army and got multiple degrees. I returned to that teacher and spoke to the class and the High school assembly. That same teacher became vice principal. I stated this closing point. "The opinion of someone else should never be greater than the opinion you have of yourself."

Since that time, I've faced many personal challenges, saw a few more "fortune tellers" along the way and have been tested to the very core of who I think I am, how much did and didn't I believe in myself and who I want to be! I have tested and examined many philosophies and theories on what a man should be and how he should represent himself personally, relationally, spiritually and socially, in order that each time I look in the mirror at myself, I am not ashamed of the image that I come to know and see. As I strive to move from being little David to big David, I want to be the man that God intended me to become.

Michelle Obama wrote a book called "Becoming," I believe her words ring true. We all are becoming who God intended us to be, as his representation here on earth. I truly believe that manhood is a process of covering and uncovering many aspects of life along the journeys that take us on an adventure of life experiences in order to teach us lessons. With every challenge, there will be a production of, joy, pain, rewards, heartache, disappointments, and accomplishments. I come to realize that in every aspect of life there will be the light of knowledge that begins to expel the darkness of ignorance. This has helped me to decrease an unwanted limitation that moves me into greater expectations of what God initially prepared for me to do, as it relates to his plan, purpose and will.

I can see in every life situation, there were multiple doors of experiences filled with wonders, mysteries and answers to unsolved questions, if I was open to receive the newness for growth. There would be and is an increase in my understanding of the term and meaning of manhood as defined by God in order for me to call myself a man. Paul stated that when I was child, I spoke like a child, thought like a child and I reasoned like a child but when I became a man, I put off childish ways. (1 Corithian 13)

I have learned that life is filled with problems, causing us to seek solutions that were designed just for me to experience a personal outcome that God wants to manifest in my life. Now many may refute this because they may not believe in God or some form of a higher power. However, life has provided me with revelation that opened my eyes to what is important. If I could turn back the hands of time, I wouldn't do many things differently because those experiences have formulated me into who I am, good, bad or indifferent.

"I can see major growth" is what I often tell my young men and boys today that I mentor or speak to in public or private sessions. I would say to them, "If I could, I live to possibly save you twenty years of unnecessary. These few gems that God has given me has truly been my pillow of peace, joy and understanding. This is true happiness as I move further into my later season of manhood. Here are a few precious thoughts that caused me to move from, living on the waves of life, to going deeper into the sea to find these pearls that many will miss. It takes work to develop the skills to be a deep-sea diver in life. Jesus wants us to be fishers of men, and that's on the surface. To truly touch the heart of man, you must be willing to go beyond the surface in order to get to the depth of the heart.

When Jesus helped the disciples become fishers of men, he was going to expose them to the proverbs of pearls that would cause them to dive deeper into their hearts and minds. To move from their traditional way of thinking to a more in-depth way of gathering knowledge, to gain understanding, bring about clarity in order to bring about the wisdom to truly become fishers of men. Like fish in the sea, they are not readily available just for the taking. Just because you believe and think they are ready for the taking. Jesus spent three years teaching them how to be fishers of men, but first he had to teach them how be men of God.

Let me share some of these pearls that took me some time to gather in the sea of life. I came to understand that becoming a man requires the youth to consider each evolving phase he will experience during the developmental process. The first phase that one must learn to understand are the various meanings of manhood through the experience from boyhood and each phase to get you toward the working definition of what is a man. Why? Because this will build a stronger foundation in order to effectively relate his derived meaning from where he is presently at, what he is developing into and beyond to others along his journey of manhood.

As boys move through the various stages of male

development, he should learn on a continuum, what he should know about his spirit housed in a body, that effects his mind and emotions. Too often, we define ourselves on a general bases therefore leaving ourselves vulnerable to unreasonable and underdefined meanings of what it means to be a man.

Therefore, we condition, train and develop the meaning of manhood in a very unstable and compromising way. This may be workable but producing underdeveloped meanings which may work in the short-term but have terrible long-term effects of what we see today. Men in adult bodies but operating from which Paul would say in the bible, thinking, reasoning and operating as a child, who hasn't really matured to their fullest potential.

Next as we begin our journey there should be a development of effective communication skills. Where the boy who is going through the evolution process understand not just verbal language but body and emotional language as well. This is essential because everything said is not always understood by the receiver of which the deliverer intended. As they would say, lost in translation.

Each of these forms of language will be vital for personal development and understanding of one's own presentation but also understanding what is presented by others. Next, one should develop an understanding of what it means to be in a relationship, starting with God, self and then others. How, who and what you are seeking in a relationship? Even more importantly, what you are willing to live with in any relationship. If you don't stand for what you truly want in a relationship from yourself and others you will fall into any kind of relationship that only uses up unnecessary time, mental, emotional and physical energy.

The reason this is significant in every relationship is because there will be many questions that will arise on how you will serve and how others will serve you? This point isn't about not being used because you are here to be used, but not misused. Therefore, you if don't have a working meaning of what a relationship should look like, it will define itself and it may not produce the outcome you as a man, or woman would seek. Therefore, producing heartache and pain that could have been avoided.

One should also learn as much about the human body as possible, understanding anatomy and physiology. Understanding the atom, molecule, cell tissue, organ and system as detailed as I presented, in collaboration with the physiological workings of the body will be essential. In order to understand how the two operate together to ensure a higher probability of optimal effectiveness throughout one's journey. For if you don't understand how to take care of the body, the body can't take care of you!

Next we should develop a better understanding of what it means to be a spirit housed in a body. We as people have been conditioned to put so much emphasis on our outer image that we have lost sight of what really drives our existence. Now I am sure many will question this thought, because there are those who don't believe in what they don't experience through their five senses. Therefore, I found on my journey that this limited me from reaching my maximum potential.

There is a much higher power that governs our lives, for it is the essences of our true source to operate in this world. If the spirit no longer lives in the body, life as we know it halts. I know this is not something we are not aware of but from how we have lived our lives, one can question how much credit we give to the spirit that dwells within. One of the best approaches I found, to really understanding the spirit man is to read, study, and mediate on the bible and pray.

The bible says in 2 Timothy 2:15 KJJV Be diligent to present yourself approved to God as a worker who doesn't need to be ashamed, rightly dividing the word of truth. The key word here is dividing the word of truth. The truth that would set you free from the bondage of worldly limitation, as it relates to people, places and things. I found once I accepted Christ as my savior and received the Holy Spirit there was a transformation of my mind, a cleansing of my heart and a renewing of my spirit.

This spiritual change didn't change me outwardly but internally because my outward presentation aligns more with the development of my internal stability. I'm becoming less preoccupied with worldly wants and desires, and more preoccupied with spiritual needs and growth. This transition is slowly stabilizing me to be a man who put off childish, worldly thoughts, to seek higher spiritual development to be a better outward and internal image of Christ.

Who displays the spiritual fruit of love, joy peace, goodness, kindness, gentleness patience, mercy, grace, forgiveness and self-control? It has been said, one is known by the fruit he bears. I believe these spiritual fruits, are truly the best nutrition to help me grow, show and be an image bearer of Christ. Therefore, being a better representation of a man, than anything the world has presented to me in my previous years on this journey.

In closing, there is much to be said about my own journey of moving from boyhood to manhood, which would take up more time and space. One thing I know for sure, I am drawing closer to becoming the man God intends me to be. The once shallow image the world defines as a man is slowly fading like a vapor that lack substance; and is now becoming a rock for which, I can stand with conviction.

I am a man who is accountable, responsible, respectful, kind, gentle, yet strong. A man who is understanding that he must constantly work on himself in order to be a blessing to someone. A man who is now a father and who better understands fatherhood and the many aspects of this role. A man who understands leadership and the responsibilities that come with it. And even more, a man who strives to be an image bearer of Christ who was the man's man. The role model, the teacher, preacher, the wisdom of one who would be King of Kings and Lord of Lords. Now I can move through the rest of my journey of manhood with a level of confidence. The word of God says, I don't have to be a cast away because there is a great recompense of rewards.

About David

David Patterson is on a mission to be a change agent in the world of youth.

With 37 years of military experience he has trained hundreds of soldiers throughout his career.

Trained in the area of counseling, fitness, resiliency and leadership, and formally educated in all three domains.

He has developed a strong foundation in communication, motivation and inspiration that has inspired others to maximize on their God given potential.

With a high level of commitment to bringing diversity into the youth forethought, teaching the youth to not be a time consumer but a future producer.

Emphasizing Education, Self-development, Community and Spiritual connection, he sees a future transition of youth, working in harmony and changing the world one individual at a time.

David lives in Michigan.

Connect with David: derome7@yahoo.com

Pain is Necessary

DOMMARTINI SALIEN SR

"The more you love, the more you suffer."
Vincent Van Gogh

Growing up in the Caribbean islands as an eight-year-old boy afforded me the most ethereal and priceless memories of my boyhood. I can remember the times that myself, my younger brother Coby, and my late cousin Jerry, (may he continue to rest in power), would be out in the shanty slum neighborhoods of the Delma district, running around, trying to catch field mice to domesticate them. Or the times we would find a couple of empty car tires, and one of us would sit inside the tire while someone else would push us down a small hill. Those were happier times. Those were peaceful times. Those were simpler times. I was such a carefree and naïve child. Although I was not fully aware of it, during that era, the country of Haiti was being ruled by a brutal despot by the name of Duvalier, who was bent on eradicating any opposition to his government among its citizens.

My father was an educator at the largest university system in the country. He was, and still is to this very day, a distinguished intellectual with the heart of a fierce lion who disagreed with the government and often spoke out about it without reservation in his lectures to his students. Duvalier had a brutal militia group known as the Tonton Makout that would circulate the country, ensuring that anyone who opposed him verbally, politically, economically, etc., was silenced permanently. I was completely oblivious to what was going on with that aspect of my life because I was too busy enjoying the priceless things in life: my youth, good friends & family, uninhibited nature, great food, and a rich collectivist culture.

Hence the extreme confusion, frustration, and immense sadness I felt when I found out abruptly one day that we, as a family, were going to be leaving Haiti, the only thing that I knew and understood, and migrate to the U.S., by way of Miami Florida, with no intent of ever returning. I remember that moment like it was yesterday. Where were we going to be living? What was life going to be like? Why were we leaving in the first place? These were questions that neither of my parents seemed to want to share the answers to. Nothing made much sense from that moment on, and somehow, I knew that my life was about to change in the most radical way possible, and an undeniably unique and universal force would be the prominent guide throughout all of it.

Pain

We landed at Miami International Airport in the fall of 1988. I vaguely remember the exact moment of landing on U.S. soil; however, I do remember my first immediate culture shock. You see, there were no 'fast food' restaurants anywhere in Haiti when I was growing up, zero. So, the first time I ever saw people standing in a literal line waiting to give someone behind a counter money in exchange for food that they made for them in less than a few minutes absolutely blew my mind. I thought this would be the end of the level or degree of shock, but I was sorely mistaken. My father shared with us that the family members we thought we were going to be boarding up with until he and my mother could stand up on their feet grew cold feet and wouldn't welcome us into their homes, which meant we were going to be homeless, and by homeless I mean a husband, wife, & two kids with absolutely no one to turn to for help, no income, sleeping underneath an avocado tree for a few days before we were finally able to stay with a friend of my father.

The memories of living with my father's friend are somewhat a blur, but I do remember the first time my mother got mugged and assaulted, not too far from there, in broad daylight, right in front of me and my little brother. One minute, we were walking down the sidewalk, and I was holding one of the stroller handles that my mother was pushing my little brother in, and the next minute, a man was attempting to pull my mother's purse away from her. The entire time she was shrieking for help as she and the assailant were fighting with the band of her purse, I stood there, completely frozen, while my little brother sat sobbing his eyes out in his stroller.

It was as though I was witnessing a scene from one of those American drama shows I used to watch back in Haiti and wondered to myself, how do people let other people treat them this way on purpose? Realizing that my mother was not going to quit putting up a fight for her purse, the robber punched her square in the face with such force that it threw her onto the sidewalk curb, and as quickly as he showed up, he vanished down the street, purse in tow. Amidst the chaos, somehow, my little brother managed to free himself from the seat buckle of his stroller and accidentally fell face flat on the hard concrete, which sent his body into a semi-shocked state. I ran over to help him off the ground as my mother was coming to. I don't know why any of this happened, but I'm kind of glad it did.

Indulge me for a brief moment to explain why I made that statement. No, when this incident happened, I was not happy, nor did I feel safe. I was, in fact, terrified, traumatized, shocked, hurt, confused, and filled with shame for not doing anything...for simply standing there. **Looking back in hindsight,** I am glad it happened the way it did (no one was seriously injured or killed) because it gave me my first taste of the realities of living in America and to realize that my childhood, adolescence, and even adulthood would be marred by something that I have come to consider my life's greatest friend.

Pain

The Spring of 1997 was the first time I ever considered giving up on this phenomena called living. It was a usual Sunday morning. My father and mother were up bright and early along with me. My little brother and baby sister at the time were just beginning to wake up to the loud Celine Dion music my mother was playing and singing to in the living room. I was sitting at the small dinette table eating cereal, admiring my mother's passion, vocal expression, and overall love for living. I have never known her to have an angry bone in her entire body. As a matter of fact, I don't remember her ever expressing any uncomfortable emotion towards me or my siblings.

My father was the disciplinarian between the two, so she would always try to come in to advocate for any "consequence" (code for ass whoopin) that my siblings and I were about to receive at the hands of my father. They both are boomers, so my father's style of parenting was riffed with beat first, ask questions later. Although my mother never, and I mean NEVER, interfered with my father's disciplining of us, I knew deep down she was hurt by those sessions. Don't get me wrong, my father wasn't extremely abusive. However, he did have a lot of unhealed and unresolved childhood traumas that he couldn't help but pass down to us growing up in Haiti. There was something about moving to the U.S. that seemed to make it that much worse. Whenever my mother would pop her cassettes in the family boombox and let Celine Dion's voice (along with her own beautiful voice) fill the rooms of the little house we lived in in North Miami Beach, the world around me seemed to stop, and all I could do was watch her live out loud.

On this obscure Sunday morning, though, something was a bit off, but I couldn't quite put my finger on it. My father was sitting on the living room couch reading the Sunday papers as usual, and now, my little brothers Coby and Steph were roaming the house for food. I didn't notice it at first, but my mother would play a certain length of a song by Celine, and then pause the song, rewind it, and then play it again. She did this a second, third, and fourth time before my father began to also take notice. She stood there motionless, doing this same thing a few more times before my father stood up to walk over to her and ask her if she was ok.

Have you ever seen a train accident video on YouTube where the car or whatever the vehicle is stuck on the tracks at the crossing? You can witness the entire accident as though it was playing at half the video speed. This was what I was witnessing, but I didn't realize it until it was all over. The moment my father touched her shoulder to see if she was alright, she let out a blood-curdling wail that seemed to come from all of the African ancestors of lifetimes past who couldn't hold back the endless pain any longer. She began speaking the verse section of the song she was playing, pausing, rewinding, and playing over and over again. She started staring at my father while doing so with eyes devoid of anyone I had considered to be my mother. It was as though a complete stranger had entered into her body and was in complete control. She began ripping at her clothes, managing to rip off half of her top as well as her skirt, revealing her undergarments.

My father somehow seemed to also go into an automated mode as he immediately grabbed my baby sister, little brother, and me by the arm and quickly ushered us out the front door onto our screened-in porch with one hand while he still remained inside attempting to fight this woman I once knew as my mother off of him. My siblings were, of course, hysterical with tears. While I can remember, there was a certain calm within me the entire time all of this was taking place. He closed the door behind him, and I could hear the furniture moving. This other individual in there with him was making sounds I didn't think were possible for any human to make. Suddenly, my basketball came crashing through the living room window, shards flying everywhere. I grabbed the doorknob and cracked it open to peer in and see what was going on, and I stood there absolutely frozen at what I saw. There.....standing there half-naked, covered in blood, panting ferociously with raw frenzy in her eyes, was my mother holding a piece of the broken glass from the window, attempting to stab my father with it.

I immediately closed the door, and the scuffling continued for what felt like an eternity, but it was only a few minutes. Suddenly, there was complete silence. My father stepped outside, closed the door behind him with the cordless phone in his hand, and walked us all out into the front yard while making a phone call. He phoned a family friend to pick us up and take us with him while he waited for 911 to arrive. I remember sitting in the back seat of the friend's car, looking out the side window as we drove away. I remember the look on my father's face as he turned to head back inside the front porch. It was a look that will forever be seared into my memory, and I will probably take it with me into the next lifetime. What I saw on his face was the same thing I felt then but could not put into words.

Pain

It's been said that those with a big heart and deep intelligence are destined to live a life of absolute and inevitable pain. I think this is a true and accurate statement. Looking back on my life in the last four-plus decades and weighing out the joyful times against the painful times, I have to say I really can't say I have more joyful memories than painful ones. The memories that brought smiles to my face are almost completely overshadowed by those that kept the tears flowing. As a human, I have often wondered why "bad" things happen to "good" people. I honestly don't think there is a sufficient enough response to that question, nor will it ever be. It's pretty simple as to why:

Pain

Is

Necessary.

Pain is the absolute contrast to joy, and because the only true value that explains the beauty of life is balance, one cannot expect a life filled with nothing but one of any of the following (but not limited to):
Love/hate
Happiness/sadness
Strength/weakness
Friends/enemies
Beauty/ugliness
War/peace

To live on purpose and to live in purpose is to try to live in balance with all that is. As I sit here and pen these very words, it has given me the space I did not think I needed to release some of these childhood traumas and continue to heal the inner me. I sincerely hope that you, beautiful reader, can reflect and recognize in your own life where you are, where you have come from, and where you aspire to see yourself in the unknown future. Whatever you discover, remember it's all part of the process.
Peace and blessings.

About Dommartini

Dommartini Salien, Sr. (aka Martini). is a first-generation immigrant from the island nation of Haiti. He migrated to United States in the late 80's with his parents and younger brother by way of South Florida.

Martini completed K-12 in South Florida, and later went on to enlist in the U.S. Army as a Logistics Specialist in 2003. After serving ten years in the armed forces, two tours in Iraq, being stationed on two continents, and traveling the world,

Martini decided to complete his military career in 2012 and pursue his undergraduate degree while simultaneously working for multiple companies in corporate America. After completing his degree, Martini received a calling to make a huge career shift by becoming a middle school educator teaching brown and black kids in underserved communities.

He pursued his graduate degree in business administration as a means to launch his non-profit organization which gives brown and black kids vocational skills if college isn't a route for them.

Martini has been an educator for a total of six years and currently lives in Brooklyn, New York with his wife.

No Rite To Passage on the Journey To Manhood

CURTIS TANNER

No STOP signs, no green lights, no tolls, nor a rite to passage on the journey to Manhood. At 18 years old, the world would label you as a man. Although you are older and have some characteristics, you may look older for your age but not yet have the experience or wisdom to become the Man you want to become. The journey to Manhood is a never-ending journey. When you get to the part of your journey when you want to be better than yesterday, you're on the right path to Manhood.

Growing up in a single-parent home, I was the only boy and middle child. Having my mother as my first love and my older and younger sisters as my first best friends, I knew love and nurturing at an early age. The absence of my father for many years would soon make my journey to becoming a man tough and unpredictable. Without my father in the picture, my mother did her best to prepare me for the next level in my life the best way she knew how.

Being gentle and a gentleman to a woman was one of my first lessons from my mother. From holding the doors to pulling out chairs to lifting heavy items. Those are things that are part of my character and that I love and use on my journey. I often find myself reflecting back to my younger self and thinking about what I would have done differently. I don't have a lot that I'd say I would change if it didn't get me to the same place I am today. My journey from a boy to a man has many starting points when I think back over my years. This particular part of my journey unlocked a new part of my character.

It was the beginning of transitioning from a boy to a young man. 16 years old was a significant age in our household; we could openly speak about the relationships we wanted to have; I got my ears pierced, and we could stay up later and stay outside later as well. Cell phones were the hottest thing out, and I wanted one for my birthday. My mother made it happen. A Silver Verizon Camera flip phone and a new curfew were my gifts that year.

With the phone came new rules and new expectations, the bill not being one of them. I didn't have the phone a good two weeks before I was coming in late and breaking curfew. I knew I was getting in trouble that night. Whooping, no outside, and she's taking my phone! I'm playing all the scenarios in my head as I walk past the streetlights I was supposed to beat home before they came on. I walked in the door prepared for the worst.

My mother called me to her room with a stern voice," Curtis, you decided to come in; now come here." As I enter her bedroom, she looks and grins at me, saying," You think you grown?" I'm confused about the question. She repeats, and I answer, "No, I do not think I'm grown," she replies, "Now I think you think you're grown, coming in the house when you want and not picking up the phone." Thinking she would take my phone, she said, "Grown people pay their own bills." Shocked, but I knew she was serious when she started writing down the due date and amount. I cried then and there, "I'm not grown; I'm sorry, I can't afford to pay $25 for my phone bill; please, I'm sorry," I begged. The last words before she sent me to my room were," Figure it out"!

The next few days were very eye-opening for me. I didn't want to lose my phone so I started saving all my little coins and change I could find. The bright idea came to start seeking money in other ways as my due date approached. I got the lawn mower and the gas tank and asked if she could take me to get some gas; I wanted to try something. We go get gas, and I tell her, "I'm going around to see if I can get some grasses cut so I can pay my bills." She smiles and says be safe and be home before dark".

I go out with the mindset that I have bills to pay and I need to get to work! That day, I made about $145 from cutting yards and had more business the next day. Running home right before dark, I park my equipment and proceed to my mother's room. I greeted her with the biggest smile, and she smiled, saying "What you smiling for? How was it? I replied," How much was my phone bill again momma?" She said, "It's just $25!" But I knew that wasn't the actual amount, so I said, "I wanted the real number"; She replied, "your bill is $45". Excited to count up 45 dollars, I said, "I'll have this every 5th of the month for my phone bill."

With every step from that moment I moved, I knew I was leaving a boy's place to position myself for my journey from being a young man to being the Man I'm proud of today. There are only so many years a young man can operate and move as a boy or immaturely because age is expected to come with maturity and certain levels of wisdom that should be used.

The journey to Manhood does not come with a set of directions, nor can you GPS your way to the point of your choosing. Although the voyage will have its challenges and be tough, it is rewarding. Life is a marathon, not a sprint! Enjoy the journey and soak up the knowledge and wisdom from the journeymen ahead. Your path may get dark and scary but stay the course and stay true to what you stand for. Being selfless and noble are great traits to practice along the journey, and having integrity in everything you do will bring light to your journey.

About Curtis

Curtis Tanner is a Licensed Master Barber Stylist with a passion for people. In addition to his career as a barber, Curtis also serves as a Family Care Coordinator at Emory Hospital in Atlanta and is the King of Customer Satisfaction.

Outside of his professional life, Curtis finds joy in spending time with his family, traveling, and mentoring young men. He believes in the power of positive role models and strives to make a difference in the lives of others.

As a Brand Strategist for Pa-Pro-Vi Publishing, Curtis also helps individuals and businesses develop their brand identity and create effective marketing strategies.

With his expertise in both the barbering industry and brand development, Curtis Tanner is a multifaceted professional who brings creativity, compassion, and dedication to everything he does.

Curtis Tanner, was born in Atlanta, Georgia and is currently residing in Peachtree Corners, GA,

Welcome To My Journey

KEVIN VAUGHAN

I must start off with my grandparents and parents more than anything else, for without GOD and my family, I would not exist. First, I start with both my paternal grandparents, whom I miss, respect, and love. Part of my journey begins with Mr. Willie & Madie Vaughan, who lived in Woodland, North Carolina, and gave birth to my dad, Nathaniel Vaughan. From this side of the family, I saw family strength, family working together, and love for all the family. I saw this and remembered this, to this day, on the good life of my grandparents on my dad's side.

Some of the great things I saw and heard that helped shape me from a boy to a man was seeing the men in the family be men. The men were husbands, businessmen, and dads to their children and were not afraid to work and be good neighbors in the community. On this side of the family, I saw good times in laughter, joy, and fun, especially in the summertime when all the cousins, aunts, uncles, and friends would meet for eat, fellowship, and talk- wow, some great times; this was called the family networking. One of the most significant things I saw on my paternal grandparents' side was the sense of wanting to get married and have my own family one day- and I did.

One of my favorite scriptures from the word of God includes a familiar passage- When I was a child, I spake as a child, I understood as a child, I thought as a child: but when I became a man, I put away childish things; I Corinthians 13:11. I must state; seeing my father's side of the family over the years instilled a great urge to grow, learn and be the best person I could be from the legacy left from my paternal grandparents and father- this truly helped me move from a boy to a man that the family would love and be proud of.

Next, let me share about my wonderful maternal grandparents, whom I also miss, respect, and love. The next part of my journey includes Mr. Melzo & Bessie Rutherford, who lived in Marion, North Carolina, and birthed my mother, Laura Elizabeth Rutherford. On this side of the family, I witnessed a true sense of family strength and love. Also, an area that contributed to my success from a boy to a man was a true and applied sense of discipline- in short, I got a lot of spanking around family, friends, and church. I must state that most of my discipline growing up came from my mother's side of the family- boy, they did not play with me acting up at times. So, as I look back in retrospect, I can see that transformation process that helped me understand that one day, I would be a man, not just a man, but a man that would hopefully represent the family values that I saw within the family structure.

Now, bringing the two-family sides together, I get Mr. Nathaniel and Laura Vaughan, who, of course, born and raised me. I was born in Ahoskie, North Carolina, and raised in Poughkeepsie, New York, where my parents moved to live, purchased a house, and worked- such great memories growing up. One great memory was Christmas time; boy, we had the best Christmas celebrations ever. Many of our Christmas celebrations were at home, with family, friends, or my godparents- so special and play a tremendous role in shaping my beliefs, character, and love for the season of giving.

However, as I share my journey from a boy to a man, I also became involved in the community in positive ways. Some of these positive areas I enjoyed were completing all the levels of education up to the college level, participating in sports (track & field, football, and basketball), church activities, community activities, and having pretty good friends growing up. As I think back, another big influence was being with my dad. Dad would take me to the barbershop to get my hair cut and let me ride around with him to see some of his friends in the city.

Another thing I remember well that helped shape me from boy to man was thinking that Dad knew everyone in the city. As a boy, no matter where we drove, he knew someone and others knew him. I mainly witnessed people knowing my dad at work and around Poughkeepsie- it was pretty cool; this was one of the areas where I wanted to be like Dad- knowing many people. To this day, in my personal life and business life, I know many wonderful people who have helped influence my manhood journey each day I live.

Finally, and in sharing, one crucial area of growth for me was the spiritual side of the family. Of course, I didn't really see or understand the spiritual areas as a boy, but now I do as a man. I can genuinely pull all my family experiences and understandings that led me to truly cherish and understand the importance of believing in God, His Son, and later the Holy Spirit. My family, both sides, knowingly and unknowingly, had a tremendous role in shaping my spiritual journey from boyhood to manhood- this I will never forget and will be eternally grateful for.

"Welcome to my future," Kevin A. Vaughan.

About Kevin

Kevin Vaughan is an engineer with Bachelor of Science Degree in Electronic Engineering Technology, and a businessman and CEO/Founder of the Men's Let's Talk Network (MLTN), LLC.

Kevin resides in Kennesaw, Georgia, with his beautiful wife of four-three (43) years- Denise. Kevin's background in engineering includes forty (40) years of working for four (4) of the top aerospace and missile defense companies in the world. Additional training and certifications include experience and a great resume in quality engineering, quality control, and quality assurance policies, procedures and systems.

In the business world, Kevin commands a global podcast and streaming service network using the latest technologies to meet the client and customer needs for business, communication, and branding. His business network is global and reaches ten (10) countries for business, teaching, training and networking.

The main focus of the business sector is to promote the B.E.T.T brand. The B.E.T.T. branding deep dives into business, education, training, and technology; these all are used and incorporated into a business model for clients and customers.

Kevin's business network also uses ten (10) social media platforms to promote the MLTN brand of products, goods, and services. One of Kevin's favorite quotes is "Welcome to Your Future".

Crushed Glass

ANTHONY WALLACE

As a little boy I had no safe place to walk. Barefooted and unprotected from the crushed glass that would cut me from every angle in my feet. The floor wasn't swept as I cried and screamed walking on this crushed glass. l can still see it In my dreams! My mom was so young when she met my dad, it wasn't even a relationship but something closer to a one-night stand! As the two came together to have their quick feeling of pleasure, a pregnancy would surface!

She would go back to the bar where she met my dad to tell him of her pregnancy but he would look at her and ask her who the lucky man was. A response she wasn't looking for from him but when she told him that he was, he took his drink, tossed it in her face and walked away! There she stood, humiliated with tears pouring from her eyes like a waterfall. She walked out of the bar, completely embarrassed and filled with resentment!

The foundation that was set for me would be a floor filled with crushed glass. This life of crushed glass would represent the mistakes I would make not having two nurturing parents to walk with me through life! My mother never wanted me. When I was seven years old, she told me she tried to abort me using a coat hanger. Her plan was to kill me, her unborn fetus! She decided not to abort me but she still wanted to give me away! What kind of thing is this to tell a seven-year-old child, or any child? After I was born, she told me I was such a beautiful baby but she still had mixed emotions whether she wanted to keep me or not.

After some time had passed, she ran back into my biological father at the bar and he asked her about me! She told him I was dead and then walked away! I suppose at that moment that was her payback after he threw a drink in her face when she told him she was pregnant with me. The crushed glass was lying on the floor way before I took my first step. The crushed glass was sharp and shiny, ready to pierce and puncture every angle I will walk through in life! My mother would see my father again but this time, she asked him to follow her. He followed her to where I was and as soon as he laid eyes on me, he began to cry because I looked just like him! After that, he would only come around a few more times but then he disappeared like a cloud of smoke into thin air! He would leave my mother with the responsibility of trying to raise a son without a father!

I believe this was one of the sharpest pieces of glass that would cut not only my feet but my heart! The absence of a father gives a child a lack of security and safety! My mother was such a young mother. She was only seventeen years old when I was conceived. She had no guidance and no real male role models in her life! She was constantly in search of love, something that she never received from my grandfather!

My mother and grandmother would often fist fight! The dysfunction between them was great! My mother would find herself in search of love as a tiny ship sailing into the ocean without any direction! Her search would land her on an island of more pain and confusion which would be with a man who was more into the streets than he was her. Her decisions with men would also be another piece of crushed glass that would nearly cripple me for life!

When I was three, my mother decided to give me away to my uncle's girlfriend. After six months, my mother had a change of heart and came back to get me. This broke my uncle's girlfriend's heart. I can't remember my time with her but I know she loved me. She would weep for days missing me because the bond would be broken between us. Meanwhile, my father was strolling through life without taking care of me. He went on to have more children, even left Cincinnati and moved to California. It was as if for him, I didn't exist.

Ever since l could remember, I felt like something was missing in my life, a presence that I needed. As I grew older, I realized what was missing was a father! having the need of a father is one piece of glass that would stay stuck in my foot for more years than l care to remember! At the age of seven l remember my mother telling me the man l was calling Daddy wasn't my daddy. l was so puzzled! l would ask questions all the time about my dad which would irritate my mother. l believe it was partially because she didn't have the answers to my questions. When she told me at seven that she wanted to abort me, I remember walking out of her bedroom feeling unloved with tons of questions because I didn't understand; after all I was just a child.

The glass of abandonment from my father was deep but the glass of having a mother who thought of murdering me was something that made me cry myself to sleep as a little boy.

Who was I?

Who did I look like?

Where was my dad?

The questions began to overwhelm my little mind as my heart felt an emptiness l couldn't explain! All these pieces of glass enabled me to grow properly and shook the very foundation of my youth.

As if things were not already bad, my mother met Mr. Tyrant. He started out seemingly kind and caring. It was enough to make my mother feel safe as if she had found the man of her dreams. However, my grandmother saw right through him. She tolerated him but didn't care for him at all. This man created so much crushed glass for my life. Instead of teaching me, he enjoyed watching me walk through it with laughter and excitement, as l screamed for help to teach me how to be a man! His kindness wouldn't last long. It would be evident that he wasn't interested in showing me anything but to display characteristics of a true abusive man and narcissist.

My little hands were raised, I was wanting to be picked up as l looked down at the floor of life. The sparkling sharp pieces of glass would continue to cut me. There was no one to lift me out of the painful place I would continue to walk, only to leave behind a trail of blood, meaning bad decisions. Growing up in dysfunction was normal to me. The beatings I would see Mr. Tyrant give to my mother was a wide sharp piece of glass that cut from one side of my foot to the other. My mother literally became a punching bag! She seemed afraid, but in love with him at the same time and l couldn't understand why!

Why would she stay?

One day, he relentlessly punched her in the face and she flew back and hit her head on a wooden table leg! The sharp glass of trauma had tears pouring down my face, as if each tear was in a race to hit the floor. Another sharp piece of glass that I would encounter would be the influence of alcohol. I would often see my mother and Mr. Tyrant drinking. The first person that would ever get me drunk would be my grandmother! I can remember her telling me and my siblings not to tell our mother. The sharp glass of alcohol would cloud my vision and numb my feelings. I would grow to fall in love with a substance that didn't love me!

I remember my stepfather Mr. Tyrant taking me for a ride with a 12-pack of Wiedemann beer. He was passing me beers as he was driving around. l liked the buzz feeling, the taste was strong and the beer was cold. This was surely setting me up to fail because he was training me to like something my underage self wasn't supposed to even have. I was around eleven or twelve years old when he smoked a joint with me. This was a different feeling. I felt like everything was moving in slow motion! It was like I could see people talking but I couldn't hear their words! This addiction would be the hardest piece of glass I would ever have to get out of my feet if I was ever going walk through life correctly! How can I walk through life as a young man with an un-swept floor filled with glass. The path was paved with pain after pain. My choices were already made for me! I had no coach, no mentor, nobody to sweep the crushed glass out of my path, so I often stumbled and fell into mischief.

At age thirteen, the glass of suicide would almost destroy me. I stepped on this glass feeling helpless and worthless! By this age, my stepfather was ruling our household with an iron fist! Often times I felt like target practice. He could shoot his anger and torment me however he pleased. He loved punishing me. Oftentimes I would be on punishment for the most ridiculous reasons. I remember clearly the day I went into the bathroom medicine cabinet and grabbed a handful of pills. I took them with tears in my eyes hoping not to wake up. I woke up looking around and saying to myself, "that didn't work!" Depression would be another piece of glass that would sever me from tranquility. Throughout the years, the glass of a confused mind, trying to find my way, would cut me more times than l can count.

One day, my mother had enough, she decided she was leaving Mr. Tyrant. She waited for him to leave, gathered us all up and we ran to get on the bus! For a brief moment, l felt a sigh of relief! My mother took us to a battered women's shelter where we stayed for several days. It was a lot of fun and my mom promised us she would never go back to him; but that was a lie! She went back to him a few weeks later. l remember feeling helpless and deceived! At that point, l realized it didn't matter what he did, she would always love him. l felt her love for him was deeper than her love for me. This was also another deep piece of glass cutting me! For years, l would go through life constantly walking through glass, even when l didn't have to but the glass was all l had ever known!

It's a sad reality when dysfunction is all we can function in. My teenage years would be horrible! I saw crack cocaine take complete control of my stepfather and mother! Our house became a crack house. This glass was so deep, it affected us all, sending our entire household into a catastrophic situation!

How could l walk through life without all of the necessary

tools to survive? The scars on my feet would be constant reminders of life's painful lessons without a guide! My adult life would be filled with anger, mistakes, and a long list of bad choices! Although I was of adult age, I had not fully grown into the mature man l needed to become! I would journey through life longing for acceptance. living in constant doubt of myself. I questioned as to whether l could ever measure up to becoming the man l had never seen!

Why couldn't l be raised by a father and a mother who loved me?

Why couldn't my path be smooth as new concrete?

For years it seemed to hurt me to breathe! I inhaled feeling of regret as l exhaled a feeling of misery!
When would l see that love I needed would never be found in a liquor bottle but only in God and myself? If I'm honest about it, even as a fifty-year old man, at times l still struggle. l can see the scars on my feet from all the crushed glass l had to walk through. The glass of low self-esteem kept me running in circles with people who were toxic! It kept me hanging out in dangerous situations! All the negative voices inside my head kept telling me l would always be that little boy who was made to walk in crushed glass!

The freedom would come in a way I never expected! It came from a church invite at the age of eighteen! It was a feeling l will never in my life forget! I heard a preacher say words that spoke to my soul! After he preached, l found myself at the altar! Before l knew it, l was being baptized and it was one of the best feelings l had in the world! It was as if l could feel a hand wiping me off from my head down to my toes! It was like l could fly! No feeling could ever compare to this feeling! Once I experienced Christ Jesus, the crushed glass l walked on all my life, seemed to have a purpose.

About Anthony

Anthony Wallace is an author, poet, and motivational speaker. He is the author of several children's books, including "From Fears to Friends", "My Neighbors Don't Look Like Me!", and "Ouch Lies Hurt!" As a child, Anthony lived a nightmare that he thought he would never wake up from. Anthony writes human interest books that come from years of personal experience. Each book has nuggets of hope and positive fragrances of peace.

"Will Somebody Please Teach Me How To Be A Man?" is Anthony's fifth book. His vision with this book is to make a difference in the lives of fatherless children who seek the guidance of a dad. His prayer is that this book will serve as a tool to unlock the door to healing and freedom!

Anthony loves to encourage and inspire. Reach out to him if you need encouragement. May your life develop into who God desires for you to become. Anthony is a native of Cincinnati, Ohio but resides in College Park, Georgia.

Email: aw124541@gmail.com

From The Desk of the Publisher

LaQuita Parks- Publisher

My Story!

Trust in the Lord with all your heart; and lean not to your own understanding. In all your ways acknowledge Him and He shall direct your paths. Proverbs 3:5-6 NKJV

My story started when I was a little four-year-old girl who went into the hospital to have her tonsils removed. It was supposed to be a "simple procedure!" While I was recovering overnight from the successful tonsillectomy, a nurse came into my room and jabbed me in the thigh with a needle filled with penicillin. I was the wrong patient! By the time my mother got back to the hospital from checking on my two sisters, they were rushing me to the OR to amputate my leg.

This started a medical Sunami that has affected my life for the last fifty- years and will affect my life for the rest of my life.

In 2016, I wrote and published my first book titled, "Walking Limitations" by Other People's Definition!" This is my true story of how I was crippled for life at the hands of a nurse. To quote my favorite verse in the poem by Langston Hughes called, "Mother to Son", "life for me ain't been no crystal stair." Life for me was tough but there was something inside of me that would not allow me to quit, no matter how difficult things got. Although I knew my father, he was not in the home. In fact, he was in the military and never lived in the same city as we lived.

As I got older, I started to realize that there was healing in sharing, so I started to share my story as I listened to others share theirs. I also began to recognize that I was behaving like a victim (even though I was) I didn't like people to have pity on me because it made me feel like I was a weak link, so I became even more determined to help others.

In November of 2019, I had to spend some time at the Mayo Clinic (still dealing with the medical Sunami) and while I was there, I had people calling me and asking me if I could help them with their book project. My first thought was "I'm at the Mayo Clinic, I can't help you with your book" but instead of saying what I was thinking, I said yes. I ended up publishing a couple of books while I was making trips back and forth to the Mayo Clinic and I found that it took my mind off of what I was going through. On my last trip to the Mayo Clinic in February 2020, my doctor looked at me and said that he was sorry for the pain that I have endured and will continue to endure, but while I may be suffering, the good news was that I wasn't dying. Although this was good news and bad news at the same time, I knew that suffering could not be my life.

There was nothing I could do about my condition, what happened to me was not my fault. I could have sat down and had myself quite the pity party, but I wanted more for my life. I wanted a quality life. In the midst of all this, my phone continued to ring with people wanting me to help them write and publish their stories. In August 2020, in the midst of the pandemic, Pa-Pro-Vi Publishing LLC was born.

Pa-Pro-Vi means Pain, Progress, Victory because I believe that without pain there is no progress and without progress there can be no victory. I help people take their stories from a "thought to a realization!" 100% of everyone living and dead has a story. At Pa-Pro-Vi, I provide a professional, productive platform for these individuals to share their story and start the healing process. I have the honor of working with some amazing people who have some amazing stories and the men in this book are no different.

There is someone waiting on the other side of these true stories so they can get healing from their story. So, you...yes you...what are you waiting for? What's your story? Book a discovery call with me today and let us help you take your story from a "thought to a realization!"

www.paprovipublishing.com

About LaQuita

LaQuita is the Founder and CEO of Pa-Pro-Vi Publishing and A Failure 2 Communicate LLC as well as a Relationship Communication Coach, Writing Coach and Mentor with a passion for people and their well-being. She is also the host of her own podcast show, "My Heart on Pages" and the host of "The Power of YOUR Story" radio show. LaQuita is also the Founder and Facilitator of EXHALE-a social communication group for women who meet to discuss different issues, ranging from personal to political.

Walking Limitations is LaQuita's first published book and the true story of how she went into the hospital to have a simple procedure and it left her crippled for life at the hands of a nurse. This created a medical tsunami that has affected her life for the last forty-nine years.

LaQuita created the Pa-Pro-Vi Publishing platform to help people start the healing process because she believes there is power in YOUR story and that writing and sharing your story can be therapeutic. Since starting Pa-Pro-Vi Publishing in 2020, LaQuita has been able to help clients all over the country take their stories from a "thought to a realization."

LaQuita also has a degree in Business and has been planning and facilitating successful mentoring and communication coaching sessions for nearly twenty years throughout the

State of Georgia and in Duluth, Minnesota

LaQuita is a faithful Christian who enjoys teaching bible study. She was baptized into Christ in 2008. She is a mother of three adult children and Nanna to 5 little heartbeats. LaQuita is a self-published author of several books including her semi autobiography titled Walking Limitations by Other People's Definition, and two children's books, she has also been featured in various magazines, and interviewed on numerous TV Networks, radio, and podcast platforms. LaQuita is an award-winning publisher and a 4x #1 International Best-Selling Author.

LaQuita lives in Riverdale, Ga and has been a member of the Forest Park Church of Christ Congregation since 2008.

Connect with LaQuita:
Facebook: https://www.facebook.com/laquita.parks.3/
Instagram: https://www.instagram.com/paprovipublishing/
Twitter: https://twitter.com/AFTC_LaQuita
Linked In: https://www.linkedin.com/in/laquita-parks-a03647a/
Website: https://paprovipublishing.com/
Email: laquita@afailure2communicate.com
paprovipublishing@yahoo.com

www.ingramcontent.com/pod-product-compliance
Lightning Source LLC
Chambersburg PA
CBHW061438030726
47503CB00005B/1466